Kate twirled, letting Tyler see her outfit. He examined it closely, seeming to be particularly interested in the shiny sequins that were sewn onto her dress.

"It's very pretty," he said. "Your wings are not like the others'."

"Thanks," said Kate. "I wanted it to be different."

"I don't know if the queen will like it," Tyler responded.

Kate was taken aback. "The queen?" she said. "Why wouldn't she like it? And what difference does it make if she doesn't? It's my costume, not hers."

Tyler looked around nervously. "You shouldn't say things like that," he told Kate. "You never know when someone from her court is near."

Kate put her hands on her hips. "Okay," she said. "This is getting a little silly. I'm really glad you're into this masquerade idea, and I know we're all supposed to be playing out the faerie thing, but come on. Your mother isn't *that* scary."

"We should walk," Tyler said, ignoring her comment. "Come with me."

Follow the Circle:

circle of three

BOOK
5

In the Dreaming

Isobel Bird

AVON BOOKS

An Imprint of HarperCollinsPublishers

Library of Congress Catalog Card Number: 00-109985
ISBN 0-06-447295-7

First Avon edition, 2001

❖

AVON TRADEMARK REG. U.S. PAT. OFF. AND IN OTHER COUNTRIES,
MARCA REGISTRADA, HECHO EN U.S.A.

Visit us on the World Wide Web!
www.harperteen.com

CHAPTER I

"This is it," Kate said, getting out of the car.

Cooper and Annie climbed out and looked around. The cabin they had pulled up in front of was surrounded by pine trees. Behind it, the woods gave way to a sandy beach, and a short dock stretched out into the gently rolling waters of the lake. The cabin itself was small and painted white, with green shutters at the windows. It belonged to Kate's family, and the three friends were using it for the weekend.

"The lake might be warm enough for swimming," Kate said. "And there's a rowboat up by the house if we want to paddle around."

Annie checked her watch. "The ritual starts at six," she said. "We should probably eat something and get dressed."

"Okay," Cooper said as they made sandwiches in the cabin's little kitchen a while later. "Tell me about what's going on tonight. All I really know is that there will be a bunch of witches and pagans running around. Did Tyler tell you anything else?"

Kate shook her head. "Not really," she said. "He was kind of secretive about it. He just said that lots of different covens get together and do a lot of fun stuff. It all seems to center around this dance in the woods, which is why Sophia told us to make costumes. But that's all I know about it."

"I see you dyed your hair for the occasion," Annie commented as she gave Cooper's pale green hair an approving glance.

"It seemed sort of Midsummery," Cooper said. "Not that I really know much about what Midsummer really is."

"I looked that up," Annie said, clearly pleased that someone was giving her a chance to show off her recently acquired knowledge. "Midsummer is the longest day of the year, which also means it's the shortest night. Pagans also call it Litha, although I couldn't really find out what that means. I think it must have something to do with light."

"That's it?" Cooper said. "That doesn't sound like anything to make a big fuss about."

"Tell it to the old witches who made up the Wheel of the Year," Annie replied. "I didn't do it."

"I'm sure we'll learn more about it when we get to the gathering," Kate said. "And I'm sure it will be interesting. Every other sabbat celebration we've been to has been."

That was true. The three friends had only experienced two of the eight sabbats, or holidays, that made up what was called the Wheel of the Year, but both of those sabbats had had unforgettable results. At Ostara, the sabbat commemorating the beginning of spring, they had met two people who quickly became important in their lives. One was Sasha, a runaway who had later been taken in by a member of a local coven. The other was Tyler. He was Kate's boyfriend—for now. She'd broken up with someone else to go out with Tyler, and recently a kiss between Kate and this ex-boyfriend, Scott, had raised some doubts in Kate about her feelings for Tyler. At the May Day sabbat of Beltane, Cooper had had her own experience with the power of magic when she'd come face-to-face with a dead girl who had been haunting her dreams, dragging them all into a roller coaster of an adventure that had culminated in Annie's kidnapping and the unmasking of the girl's murderer.

Now they were about to celebrate the third sabbat of the year and a day they had committed themselves to studying with their Wicca class. School had ended for the year only a few days ago. Finals were behind them, and they had the long, lazy summer to look forward to. Starting it off with a celebration with their Wiccan friends was the perfect beginning to what was sure to be a great couple of months. They'd each been working on a costume for the big event, and now it was time to show one another what they'd decided to be.

"What do you think?" asked Cooper, showing

Annie what looked like a short green dress covered in artificial leaves and flowers.

"Now I understand the green hair," Annie replied. "But what are you supposed to be, the Not-So-Jolly Green Giant?"

"I'm a wood nymph," Cooper said, holding up the dress. "I'm going to put leaves and flowers in my hair, too."

Annie looked doubtful. "I never really thought of you as the nymph type," she said.

Cooper reached into her bag and pulled something out. It was a flute. She played a few notes on it. "I'm the kind of nymph who leads people astray in the woods by tempting them with music," she explained. "I never thought taking those stupid flute lessons when I was nine would pay off."

Annie shook her head. Cooper just wasn't the spritely, sunshiny type. There was always an edge to her. She couldn't be just a nymph; she had to be one with an attitude. That was okay, though. Annie had made a rather unusual costume choice as well. She opened the box she'd made Cooper pack so carefully and reached inside. She lifted out the mask she'd spent all week making out of papier-mâché and then carefully painting.

"What is *that* thing?" said Kate.

The mask Annie held in her hands looked like a giant pincushion. It had a short, rounded snout, and long points of rolled-up newspapers protruded like spikes all around it. The entire thing was painted in various shades of brown.

"I'm going to be a hedgehog," Annie explained, putting the mask over her head so that it settled on her shoulders. She peered out at Kate and Cooper through the two small eyeholes above the snout.

"You're going to be a hedgehog?" Kate repeated doubtfully.

Annie nodded, her spiked head bobbing up and down. "I was reading about traditional Midsummer festivities in this book I got from the library," she explained. "In some parts of Britain the people dressed up like forest animals and held parades through the streets. I thought it sounded cool."

"Don't you dare make fun of my nymphiness while you have that thing on," Cooper said.

"You're both way too weird," commented Kate as she fetched her own costume out of her bag. Like Cooper's, it was a short dress. Only it was made of glittery pink material that sparkled when it moved. And attached to the back was a pair of short wings.

"You *would* be a faerie princess," Cooper remarked.

"And why not?" Kate demanded. "Besides, *A Midsummer Night's Dream* was the last thing we read in English before the end of the year. It seemed fitting."

"Well, we'd better hurry and get ready if we want to be on time for this thing," Annie said, taking off her hedgehog mask and picking up a sandwich.

They ate quickly, then got to work getting

dressed. Kate was the official makeup person, and she expertly applied color to Cooper's face and then her own. Because she was wearing a mask, Annie was spared being painted, but she did have to put on the shirt and pants she'd chosen to go with her costume. When she was done and had put her mask back on, she looked like a giant hedgehog dressed in a person's clothes.

"That's sort of creepy," Kate said, surveying the finished product.

"I think it's cool," said Cooper. "How do I look?"

"Like a wood sprite," Annie said.

Kate had done Cooper's eyes in several shades of green, and even used green lipstick. Combined with the green hair and the garland of flowers she had on her head, Cooper looked like some kind of strange forest creature.

Cooper played a little trill on her flute, and Annie saw that even her fingernails were painted green. As for Kate, she really did look like a faerie. Her face was made up in pinks and reds, and she had applied sparkly glitter to her skin. She'd woven pink ribbons through her hair, and she was wearing a garland of roses. The wings attached to her dress shook gently when she moved, and her dress seemed to shimmer in the light.

"We look fabulous," she declared. "Let's go."

They left the cabin and walked up the road, following the directions given to them by Tyler. At first they felt a little self-conscious, but soon they ran into other people walking along the road dressed in costumes, and they knew that they were going in the right direction. They also began to see tents of various colors scattered throughout the woods.

"Do you recognize any of those people?" Annie asked Cooper and Kate as several gaily dressed women and men passed them, laughing and singing.

"No," Kate said. "But it would be hard to recognize anyone in costumes like these. I doubt Sophia or Archer or any of the witches from the coven will even know it's us."

Ahead of them a hand-painted sign reading FAERIE GATHERING hung from a tree. The sign had an arrow pointing down a path, so they turned onto it and followed it through the woods. It wound through the trees, finally opening into a large clearing in which dozens of costumed people were standing.

"This is amazing," said Cooper as they looked around. They'd been to gatherings before, but none of them had been like this. Everywhere they looked there were women and men in beautiful, sometimes outlandish, outfits.

Annie pointed to a man dressed as a fox, with pointy ears, glued-on whiskers, and a fluffy red tail emerging from the seat of his green pants. "See," she said triumphantly. "I'm not the only animal here."

And she wasn't. In fact, there were many people dressed as animals, including a frog, an owl, a bear, and two little kids dressed as butterflies who ran around the clearing chasing one another.

"There's another faerie princess," Kate said huffily, pointing to a girl in a silver dress.

"Don't worry," Cooper said. "Your wings are *much* nicer."

As they looked around they spotted a few people they knew. But before they could go over to speak to them a trumpet sounded and there was a flurry of excitement at the other side of the clearing as a group of people walked in. In the center of the group was a tall woman dressed in flowing pink robes. She carried a staff wound with flowers and ribbons, and there were more flowers in her hair. The people around her were ringing bells, playing musical instruments, and tossing flowers at the crowd.

The woman walked into the center of the clearing and stopped. Everyone ceased talking and turned their attention to her. She waited until everyone was completely quiet and waiting for her to speak. Then she smiled.

"Welcome to Midsummer!" she cried in a clear voice as the clearing erupted in applause and shouting.

"Who is she?" Kate whispered to Annie and Cooper. But they didn't know who the woman was any more than she did, and all they could do was wait to hear what she had to say.

"As you all know, this is the longest day of

the year," the woman continued. "It is also one of the most magical. But it is not the ordered magic of ritual. It is the wild magic of the woods. The wild magic of Faerie."

At this the people around her cheered and played on their instruments until she held up her hand. They became quiet. Then she went on.

"On this night the gates between the human world and the world of the Faes may be opened. But once opened they may not be shut again until the shortest night is over. Faerie magic cannot be controlled. I cannot tell you what will happen if we unlock those doors."

She paused to give the gathered people time to think about what she was saying. Then she looked slowly around the clearing, taking in the costumed crowd.

"Do you wish to open those doors, my friends?" she asked. "Do you wish to invite the denizens of Faerie into these woods tonight? Are you ready to experience the magic of the Faes?"

"We're ready!" shouted a woman to Annie's right.

"Call them," another cried.

"Yes, call them," others agreed.

The woman held up her hand, bringing silence to the clearing.

"Are there any who do not wish to have the doors opened?" she asked.

She paused, waiting for an answer. It was as if

the entire crowd was holding its breath in antici-
pation, hoping that no one would speak. When no
one did, the woman smiled happily.

"Very well," she said. "We are in agreement. I
will call them."

She held up her staff in one hand and pointed
her other hand toward the woods. "At this time of
fair midsummer," she intoned in a singsong voice,
"longest day and shortest night. Faerie magic, fill
these woods, with joyous song and laughter bright."

There was total silence after she spoke. Then,
far away, they heard the sound of bells ringing, followed by a peal of laughter.

"The doors have been opened!" the woman
cried, and everyone cheered. She raised her hand to
silence them.

"At midnight we will meet in this clearing to
dance," she said. "Until then, the woods are filled
with many forms of merriment for your enjoyment.
Go and seek them out. Return here when the moon
is in the sky and you hear the sounds of my players
playing. But be warned—the faeries are on the loose
and their queen is looking for sport. You may
encounter strange things in the woods. And if you
are not careful, the faeries may take you away with
them. Guard yourselves."

She turned and walked out of the clearing, followed by her companions. When she was gone,
Kate turned to Annie and the others.

"What was that all about?" she asked. "That

didn't seem like a ritual at all. What are we supposed to do now?"

"Don't look at me," Cooper said. "I'm just a simple wood nymph."

"Annie?" Kate said.

"I don't know either," Annie said, sounding distracted.

"What's wrong?" Kate asked her.

"My paws," Annie said. "I forgot my paws. I made these cool paws out of brown fur, and I wanted to wear them. They must be back in the cabin. I'm going to run back and get them."

"What about us?" Kate said plaintively.

Annie shrugged. "That woman said to go play in the woods," she said. "Why not try that? I'll catch up with you guys later."

She turned and walked back toward the path, leaving Cooper and Kate alone. Kate looked unhappy. Then she suddenly perked up.

"I think I see Tyler," she said, pointing across the clearing. "I'm going to go catch up with him."

Before Cooper could respond, Kate was gone.

"Great," Cooper said to no one in particular. "Now what?"

She looked around the clearing. Most of the people had wandered off into the woods. She didn't see anyone she knew, and she had no idea what was going on. This was the oddest ritual she'd ever been to. There didn't seem to be any organization to it at all.

She wanted to run after either Kate or Annie, but she couldn't decide which one she would be able to catch up with more easily. Then she heard something. It was music, a snatch of a melody that seemed to drift to her on the wind. It was an intriguing sound. She strained to hear where it was coming from, but it had disappeared.

She tried to recall what it had sounded like, but already the memory was melting away like a chalk drawing in the rain. She gave up, and had just turned to head back down the path to the cabin in search of Annie when the song came again. This time she thought that it was definitely coming from the woods to her left. Abandoning her plan to find Annie, she walked into the trees.

I might as well see who's making that sound, she thought as she left the clearing. *I can always find Kate and Annie later.*

CHAPTER 2

"Tyler!"

Kate called out to the boy across the clearing. He was dressed all in black, from his leather boots to his black pants and shirt, and he wore a mask made of shiny black feathers. He resembled a raven. Tyler hadn't told Kate what he was going to come to the Midsummer ritual as, but she knew it was him. It was the perfect costume for his tall, lanky frame, and it reflected his inquisitive, teasing personality.

The boy turned and cocked his head, looking at her quizzically for a moment. He didn't seem to recognize her. *It must be my costume*, Kate thought as she moved toward him.

A group of people cut in front of her, and Tyler was lost from view for a moment as she waited impatiently for them to go by. When they had, she saw that Tyler had turned away and was walking into the woods.

"Hey!" she called, confused. "Tyler! Wait up."

Why was he leaving? Even if he hadn't recognized her in her getup he had to have seen her waving at him. But it was almost as if he was running away from her.

Kate entered the woods where Tyler had disappeared into the trees. She had to pause a moment to let her eyes adjust to the new surroundings. Unlike the bright light that had flooded the clearing, the light that filtered through the forest canopy was more muted. The leaves that fluttered in the summer breeze threw shadows like tiny dark moths across the ground, and everything was surrounded by the pale golden glow of late afternoon. It was beautiful, but a little disorienting, and Kate almost felt as if she were dreaming.

She looked around her, trying to catch sight of Tyler. There were other people moving about in the trees, but she didn't see him anywhere. Where had he gone? It wasn't that easy to walk quickly in the woods, but apparently he had managed to get far ahead of her already. She didn't understand it. Didn't he want to talk to her?

She was irritated, and she decided to go back to the clearing and wait for Annie and Cooper. Clearly, Tyler had something else he wanted to do, and besides, it was hard to walk in the woods with her wings on. They kept getting caught on branches, and she was afraid she would tear them. She wasn't going to ruin something she'd put so much hard work into, especially for a boy who wanted to play games.

She was just about to go back when out of the corner of her eye she caught a glimpse of something black. Turning, she saw Tyler moving quickly through the trees to her left.

"Tyler!" she called, and once again he turned and looked at her, the eyes of his raven mask staring directly at her face.

Kate darted through the trees, her wings flapping as she dodged trees. This time Tyler didn't run. He waited for her to reach him.

"Thanks for waiting," Kate said sarcastically as she stopped in front of her boyfriend, although her anger at him had already dimmed. "Didn't you see me?"

"I didn't know you were looking for me," Tyler answered. His voice sounded a little raspier than it usually did, as if he had a sore throat.

"What's the matter?" Kate asked. "Did you catch a cold or something?"

Tyler shook his head.

"That's a great costume," said Kate. "Did you make it yourself?"

"The queen made it for me," he said.

Kate raised an eyebrow. "The queen?" she said. "Is that what you're calling your mother now?"

Tyler seemed to think about her question for a moment. "The queen made all of our costumes," he said.

"I get it," Kate replied. "This is all part of the whole ritual, right? Your mother is playing the

Faerie Queen or something. Well, I can't wait to see that. But for your information, I made my costume myself. Do you like it?"

Kate twirled, letting Tyler see her outfit. He examined it closely, seeming to be particularly interested in the shiny sequins that were sewn onto her dress.

"It's very pretty," he said. "Your wings are not like the others'."

"Thanks," said Kate. "I wanted it to be different."

"I don't know if the queen will like it," Tyler responded.

Kate was taken aback. "The queen?" she said. "Why wouldn't she like it? And what difference does it make if she doesn't? It's my costume, not hers."

Tyler looked around nervously. "You shouldn't say things like that," he told Kate. "You never know when someone from her court is near."

Kate put her hands on her hips. "Okay," she said. "This is getting a little silly. I'm really glad you're into this masquerade idea, and I know we're all supposed to be playing out the faerie thing, but come on. Your mother isn't *that* scary."

"We should walk," Tyler said, ignoring her comment. "Come with me."

He began to move through the trees, and Kate followed. Tyler seemed to know where he was going, but she had no idea where they were. At least she'd found him and they were together. That was the important thing. They hadn't had much time to hang out lately, what with the end of school and everything else they were involved in, and Kate had missed him. She was hoping that these couple of days in the woods would give them a chance to spend some time alone.

As they walked along she looked around her. The woods really were gorgeous. The trees stretched far above them and the ground was dotted with plants that grew in the shade of the beeches, oaks, and pines. Fallen logs covered in velvety moss and sprinkled with strangely shaped mushrooms occasionally stretched across the various paths that wound through the trees, and the air smelled of evergreens and earth. *It's not too hard to think of this place as being magical*, Kate thought as she soaked it all in.

But she wasn't able to completely enjoy being in such a beautiful place with Tyler. Something was on her mind that prevented everything from being perfect, something that had been bothering her ever since the annual school Skip Day picnic on the beach a couple of weeks before. That something was Scott Coogan. Scott was supposed to be her ex-boyfriend. She'd broken up with him because she'd wanted to be with Tyler. She'd been absolutely sure of her decision, so sure that she'd risked being shunned by the most popular kids at school. But on Skip Day, when she and Scott had taken a walk just to talk, she'd suddenly found herself in his arms, kissing him.

She hadn't told Tyler about the kiss, and as far as she knew no one else had either. Some people at her school—a lot of people, actually—knew about the kiss, thanks to the big mouth of Kate's former best friend and now biggest headache, Sherrie Adams. But Tyler went to a different school and didn't, Kate hoped, talk to anyone at Beecher Falls High. At first she'd decided not to tell him. After all, it had been just a onetime thing, a mistake that was over and done with. There wasn't any point in making Tyler upset by telling him about it. But the more she thought about it, the more she thought that maybe she *should* tell him. After all, he was her boyfriend. They weren't supposed to have secrets from one another.

She'd planned on telling him before the Midsummer gathering, but she'd been so very busy, and the timing never seemed right. But maybe now, in the woods, she could do it. Tyler seemed to be in a good, if sort of strange, mood. If she told him now, she could enjoy the rest of the sabbat without feeling guilty.

But what if he got really angry? What if he thought she'd cheated on him deliberately? She knew that what she'd done was going to hurt him. There was no way it couldn't. But he would have to believe her when she said that it had been an accident, wouldn't he? He would know that she wasn't interested in being with Scott. Tyler was the one she loved. She knew that even though neither of them had said the *L* word yet.

Maybe it's time you said that, too, she thought suddenly.

She hadn't even thought about that. Could she tell Tyler that she loved him? That was a big deal. A really big deal. Boys always freaked out when girls told them that they loved them. At least that's what she'd always heard. Would Tyler do the same thing? He wasn't like any other guy she'd ever known. If she told him that she loved him, would he suddenly turn out to be just as nervous about hearing it as other guys apparently were?

She didn't know what to do. Should she tell him about Scott? Should she tell him she loved him? The questions repeated themselves over and over in her head as she and Tyler continued to walk. If she did tell him she loved him, how would she say it? She tried to imagine herself saying the words. Even while going over them silently in her head she stumbled over them, nervous about doing it all wrong and looking like an idiot.

They were going deeper into the forest. The trees above them grew more closely together, and less light came through. But it was still warm, and even in the diminished light Kate could see clearly. *It is the longest day of the year, after all*, she reminded herself.

"So what are we supposed to do until the dance tonight?" she asked Tyler, deciding that the issue of what to say to him could wait a while longer.

"Whatever we want to," he answered. "But the queen will be out soon, so we must listen for her."

"The queen, the queen," Kate said. "I'm getting

tired of hearing about this queen. I know she's your mother and all, but what's the big deal?"

"Quiet," Tyler said, putting a finger to his mouth. "You'll get us in trouble."

Kate rolled her eyes. "Sorry," she said. "I forgot. Why did you say she wouldn't like my costume?"

Tyler stopped and turned to gaze at Kate. "Because you are so beautiful," he said. "She doesn't like it when her attendants are more beautiful than she is herself."

Finally, Kate thought, *a compliment*. Well, better late than never. And she was glad that Tyler liked her outfit. She'd worked hard on it.

"You're not such a bad-looking raven yourself," she answered.

Kate looked up into Tyler's face. The raven mask covered his eyes and nose, but his mouth was bare. He was looking at her as if he was waiting for her to do something. She leaned forward, ready to kiss him, but he pulled away and looked around nervously.

"We can't," he said. "If she sees us she will be angry."

"Your mother has seen us kiss before," Kate said, a little annoyed. She loved it that Tyler could get so involved in the spirit of the ritual, but she wouldn't mind if he broke role for just a minute or two.

"What is your name?" he asked.

"What?" Kate said. "You know what my name is."

Tyler stared at her blankly, his eyes unmoving

behind the raven mask. What did he mean, he didn't know her name? Then Kate realized that he was simply continuing with the game. That was okay. If he wanted to pretend that they were different people she could do that. She thought for a moment before answering.

"I'm Princess Goatcheese," she said, thinking of the most ridiculous name she could.

Tyler took her hand. "And I am Raven," he said.

Kate groaned. "Couldn't you come up with something a little more original?" she asked. It wasn't like Tyler to be so boring.

He didn't reply. Instead, he bent down and plucked one tiny purple violet from a clump that was growing beside a rock. He placed it in the crown of flowers Kate wore on her head.

"Now I will always be able to pick you out from among the other faeries," he said. "Not that I would need any help."

"I should hope not," Kate said. "How many other girls with wings will be at this dance anyway?"

"All of the faeries will be there," Tyler answered. "And any others the queen invites."

"Invitation only, eh?" said Kate. "I'm glad I'm on the guest list."

"You have a strange way of talking," Tyler said. "I've never heard one speak as you do."

"Speaking of talking," Kate said, "I think we need to talk a little bit before tonight."

She was ready to tell him all about Scott and the kiss. She knew that if she put it off any longer it would just get harder and harder to tell him at all. They were alone now. Later they would be surrounded by all of their friends. This might be her only opportunity for a while. Hard as it was going to be, she just had to spit it out.

She sat down on the rock that had the violets growing around it and motioned for Tyler to sit next to her. He did, peering at her with his bird face.

"Could you take the mask off for a minute?" Kate asked him. "It's kind of tough talking to someone with a beak."

"I can't," Tyler said simply.

Kate sighed. She wasn't about to argue with him when what she was going to say would probably just make him even angrier. If he wanted to talk to her with a bird mask on, that was fine. It would be easier than staring into his eyes anyway.

"There's something I need to tell you," Kate began. She chose her words carefully so that what she said next could go either in the "I love you" direction or in the "I kissed Scott" direction. Even as she paused to speak she wasn't sure which she was going to go with first.

Tyler was waiting for her to continue. She saw him watching her, not saying anything. But now that she'd started, she didn't know what to say. Should she break his heart first and then put it back together? Or should she tell him how she felt about him so that finding out about her kissing Scott wouldn't be so hard to take? Neither option seemed very appealing now that she had to pick one.

"I think you're really special," she said finally. "That's why I need to tell you that—"

She was cut off by the sound of voices coming through the forest behind them. The trees around them stirred as if a wind were blowing, and a gale of laughter, like bells ringing, floated through the air. Kate sniffed and found that the scent of flowers had surrounded them, a mixture so rich and intoxicating that it made her head swim a little.

"It's her!" Tyler said, leaping to his feet and looking around wildly.

"Who?" asked Kate, not moving from the rock.

"The queen!" Tyler told her. "She's begun her revels. We must go quickly."

The rustling in the trees grew louder. Kate stood up, dusting off her dress and straightening her wings. "Not so fast," she said. "I want to meet this queen." She knew that Rowan, Tyler's mother, would really get into playing the role of the Faerie Queen, and she couldn't wait to see her costume.

"No," Tyler said. "You can't. She'll be angry with me. And with you. We must go." He grabbed Kate's hand and tried to pull her down the path.

Kate shook him off. "What's wrong with you?" she said, a little bit angry. "This is just a game. She's not going to do anything."

The trees around them shook, sending butterflies

23

into the air. Kate could hear the voices growing closer. She wondered how many people Rowan had with her to make so much noise. She also wondered how she'd managed to get the flowery smell so strong. *She must be covered in perfume*, she thought.

"I cannot stay," Tyler said. "Won't you come with me?"

"No," Kate said firmly. "I'm not afraid of any Faerie Queen. I'm the Princess Goatcheese, remember?"

"Very well," answered Tyler. "I hope I will see you again. Be careful. She is beautiful, but she loves nothing more than to play tricks."

He turned and darted down one of the forest paths, disappearing into the trees and leaving Kate alone to meet his mother. Kate looked after him, shaking her head. *Oh, well*, she thought as she watched him go, *at least it gives me a little more time to decide what to tell him.*

"And who might you be?" a voice behind her asked. It was a woman's voice, strong and beautiful. Hearing it, Kate knew instantly whom it belonged to. She turned around and looked into the face of the Faerie Queen.

CHAPTER 3

The music was coming from somewhere ahead of her. Cooper paused, straining to hear more clearly. All of a sudden the woods, which had seemed so silent and peaceful earlier, seemed to be full of sounds. The wind sighing in the branches. The birds chirping. The murmuring voices of the other people walking by her as she stood among the trees. They all competed for attention with the beautiful music, and she was having a hard time separating out the irresistible melody she'd heard all too briefly.

Then it came to her again, a run of notes all falling over each other like children rolling down a hill and laughing. It was like nothing she'd ever heard before. Again she tried to hold it in her memory, and again it vanished before she could quite recall all of it.

All thoughts of Annie and Kate disappeared as Cooper walked among the trees, waiting for the sound to return. She could find her friends later. There was lots of time before the big dance started.

What was it—six-thirty, seven o'clock? It was still light, although the shadows were getting longer. For a moment that worried her. She didn't have a flashlight with her. But no matter. She could always go back to the cabin and get one, or surely Annie would bring one back with her. Annie was always prepared. It was usually Cooper who was flying by the seat of her pants.

The music trickled through the trees ahead of her. She walked faster, determined to find out where it was coming from and who was making it. Now she was following a narrow path that led away from the main one and into an area thick with elm trees. The pine needles that had been under her feet gave way to soft dirt and banks of hawthorn, and as she passed through a thick stand of trees she noticed that a small stream had sprung up and was running parallel to the path, winding around the rocks.

She followed the stream as it ran downhill. The music came to her from time to time, letting her know that she was going in the right direction, and she grew more and more excited as she walked. She didn't know why, but the song she heard made her feel alive, as if she'd just woken up from a long sleep. It danced in her head, calling to her with its teasing voice, and then darted away again just as she was about to grab it and hold it in her mind forever.

She pressed through the trees, ignoring the way they scratched at her face, and came suddenly into a little grove. There the stream fell over several large stones, splashing into a pool beneath them. It was almost as if someone had dropped a cauldron into the earth. Around its edge grew water plants and reeds, and at one end a large rock jutted partly into the water, breaking what otherwise would have been a perfectly circular shoreline.

Sitting on the rock was a girl. She held a flute to her mouth, and her fingers danced along its length. Her eyes were closed and she swayed as she played, her body moving along with the song that came rippling from her instrument.

Cooper stared at the girl. She looked to be about Cooper's age. Her hair was long and black and wild, and her skin was white with a rosy cast to it. She was wearing a simple white dress that left her arms bare, and there were no shoes on her long, delicate feet. One of the straps of her dress had slipped down her shoulder, but she didn't seem to notice.

"That song," Cooper said. "It's beautiful. What is it?"

Hearing Cooper's voice, the girl gasped and looked up, shocked. She looked frightened, as if she wanted to run away.

"I'm sorry to bother you," Cooper said quickly. "I didn't mean to interrupt. I just heard the music and wanted to see who was playing it."

"You heard me playing?" the girl asked, sounding doubtful.

Cooper nodded. "I was back there," she said. "In the clearing."

27

The girl didn't say anything for a moment. She seemed to be studying Cooper intently, looking at her face. Cooper saw that her eyes were the color of pale green spring leaves. Cooper wanted to say something, but she didn't know what. Then she felt the flute in her own hand. She held it up.

"I play, too," she said quickly. Part of her was afraid that if she didn't say something the girl would just leave. "I'm not as good as you are."

"Play for me," said the girl.

Cooper licked her lips nervously. She didn't know why, but she wanted this girl to like her. She wanted her to like her playing. Putting the flute to her mouth, she blew gently and played part of a song she remembered from her lessons. When she was done she dropped her hands. The girl's eyes were closed, and she was nodding.

"Yes," she said. "I see now how you were able to hear my song. There is music in you. You play well."

"Not like you do," Cooper said.

The girl smiled. "Perhaps not," she said. "But I've been playing a long time. What's your name?"

"Cooper," Cooper replied. "What's yours?"

"My friends call me Bird," the girl said. "Why don't you call me that, too?"

"Sounds good to me," answered Cooper. Bird was sort of a strange thing to call someone, but a lot of the people she hung out with went by odd names. In fact, Bird was probably one of the least peculiar ones.

"Are you here alone?" Bird asked her.

Cooper shook her head. "I came with friends," she said. "For the Midsummer ritual. Is that why you're here?"

Bird nodded. "I am also here with friends to celebrate Midsummer," she explained. "Where are yours?"

"I'm not sure," said Cooper. "Annie went back to the cabin, and I think Kate is chasing her boyfriend around somewhere. What about your friends?"

"Getting ready for tonight," Bird said, sliding off the rock and coming over to stand near Cooper. "Would you like to meet them?"

"Sure," Cooper answered. "I don't know when Kate and Annie will be back, so as long as I make it to the big dance later on tonight I'm fine."

"We wouldn't miss the dance for anything," said Bird. "The queen wouldn't hear of it."

Cooper laughed. "I can't wait to see what this queen looks like. Everyone's been talking about her. She must be something else."

"That she is," Bird told her.

"So you've been to these things before?" Cooper asked.

"Many times," said Bird.

"This is my first one," Cooper explained. "You'll have to tell me what to expect. It's all a little new to me."

Bird put her arm around Cooper. Cooper noticed that she smelled like the forest. "You never know what to expect when the queen and her people are in the woods," Bird said as she started to walk.

They left the grove with the pool in it and entered the woods. Once again Cooper found herself surrounded by a golden haze as they walked beneath the trees in the fading sun. She couldn't tell one direction from another, but Bird seemed to know exactly where they were going. She led Cooper through a series of twists and turns that seemed to Cooper to take them in circles. But Bird kept moving steadily forward until finally they passed beneath the low branches of a towering pine tree and were once again in a circle of trees.

A dozen or so people were sitting in the clearing. They all looked up at Cooper and Bird as they entered, and Cooper couldn't help but stare back. Like Bird, the others looked like wild, overgrown children. Their hair was tangled and messy, some with leaves and twigs in it. The girls wore what seemed to be tattered dresses in various colors and the boys were all in shorts and shirtless. Yet while their clothes and hair were disheveled, they didn't seem at all dirty. It was more like they had been cut from the trees themselves, their clothing and hair simply different forms of leaves and bark.

Those are really cool costumes, Cooper thought as she looked at the group. She glanced down at her own costume, which suddenly seemed overly fussy. The others looked like they lived in the forest all the time, while she felt like she was playing dress-up.

Like Bird, each of the inhabitants of the grove had an instrument. Some had flutes like Bird's, while others had percussion instruments, bells, or what looked like small fiddles. They held them in midair, as if they'd been interrupted in the middle of a performance by the appearance of the two girls.

One of the figures detached itself from the rest and walked toward Cooper and Bird. It was a guy with long red hair that hung down his back. He'd tied feathers, acorns, and other objects from the forest into his hair, and they hung about his face like ornaments on a tree. Unlike Bird's green eyes, his were deep brown, rich as the leaves that lay decomposing on the forest floor.

"Who is this?" he asked, shooting Bird a sharp glance.

"This is Cooper," Bird told him. "She heard me playing."

One corner of the redheaded boy's mouth turned up. "Did she?" he said.

"She's amazing," Cooper said quickly. "I've never heard anything like what she was playing."

"She plays, too," Bird added. "She's good."

"As good as you?" asked the boy.

Bird didn't answer. Neither did Cooper. She just looked over at Bird, who was staring at the ground. Why wasn't she saying anything? It was almost as if she was afraid of the redheaded guy. But why would she be afraid of him if they were all friends? And why did he seem to be so unfriendly? It didn't make sense.

The red-haired guy turned his attention to Cooper and smiled, which made her feel a little better. "I guess I'll just have to judge for myself," he said. "Come over here and play with us."

He turned and walked back to the others, motioning for Cooper to follow him. Cooper looked again at Bird, who nodded. "That's Spider," she said. "This is kind of his group. He's a little bossy, but he's okay."

Cooper walked over to the others and took a seat in an empty space between a guy holding a fiddle and a girl with a bell. Bird stood nearby, watching, and Spider stood in the middle of the circle, looking at the players gathered around him.

"We're just going to play," he told Cooper. "It won't be anything you know. Just join in when it feels right, okay?"

Cooper nodded. She wondered why Bird wasn't playing with them. She almost felt as if she was auditioning for something. She wanted to play well, to impress the others with her ability, but she wasn't sure what she could do. She hadn't played the flute seriously in quite a while. In fact, before digging it out to use with her costume she'd barely touched it in over a year.

There was no time to think about that, though. At a signal from Spider, everyone began to play. The air was filled with a sound unlike anything Cooper had ever heard. It was similar to the song Bird had played, but it was even more wonderful. The melody ran here and there, never going where Cooper expected it to. She was concentrating hard, trying to memorize it so that she would be able to play against it, but just when she thought it was going to do one thing it darted off in another direction completely, leaving her confused.

After a few minutes, though, she began to understand the song. It still didn't go in one direction long enough for her to really grasp it, but she thought she could follow bits and pieces of it. It was easier when she closed her eyes. Then the music almost became images, which were easier for her to focus on. She saw people dancing, moving in a circle. They moved quickly, so quickly that they were a blur. It was as if they had turned into some kind of spinning top hurtling around and around.

Hesitantly, Cooper put the flute to her lips and began to play. At first she played only a simple countermelody, her notes bouncing off the ones the others tossed into the circle. But as she became more and more sure of herself she let her song become bolder. She wove her own tune around the one that was now becoming more and more familiar to her. She could hear her music flowing with that of the others, sometimes leaping up to rise above it and sometimes moving side by side with it.

She'd never felt such a sense of connectedness while playing with other people. The closest she'd ever come was when she played with T.J. and the rest of their band, Schroedinger's Cat. But even that wasn't like this. The music she was making with the other people in the circle was other-worldly. It made her feel as if she'd been caught up in a whirlwind and spun around until she was dizzy, then dropped out of the sky onto the soft earth.

The music stopped. Cooper opened her eyes and looked around. She was sorry that the song had ended. She could still feel it inside her, calling to her to let it out again. She wanted to return to it, to run wild with it and feel once more the exhilaration of just letting go and allowing the music to take control. She looked up and saw that Spider was looking at her and smiling.

"You play well," he said. "Most people can't keep up. Even Bird had a difficult time when she first joined us, although she's become a much better player since."

"Thank you," Cooper said. "Did you write that song?"

Spider nodded. "We write all of our own songs. That one was written especially for tonight."

"You mean for the Midsummer celebration?" Cooper said. "Are you all witches?"

The kids around her laughed loudly and happily, as if she'd said the funniest thing they'd ever heard. Cooper was confused. What was so odd about asking them if they were Wiccan?

"Are you a witch?" Spider asked in return without answering her question.

"Sort of," Cooper said. "I'm studying it. I'll decide next year if I want to be initiated or not. So what are you all doing here?"

"We go where there is magic," Spider told her simply.

Cooper nodded. She still didn't know whether the other kids were witches or not. If they weren't, she didn't understand why a bunch of people her age would be at a pagan gathering if they weren't into it themselves, but she guessed it really didn't matter. She liked the music they played, and they seemed to like her.

"Is she in, then?" Bird asked abruptly.

Cooper looked at Bird. She was standing apart from the others, her flute in her hands. She was shifting from side to side nervously and looking from Cooper to Spider and back again.

"We'll see," Spider said. "The dance isn't until midnight. There are other tests we need to put her through."

"Tests?" Cooper said.

"Don't worry," Spider said. "They're nothing too difficult. Think of it more as an initiation. You know, like the one you're considering to become a witch."

There was more laughter from the others. Cooper saw Bird frown. "What are we talking about here?" Cooper asked, confused.

"We're considering letting you join our group," Spider said. "Letting you play with us at the dance this evening. But we have to be sure that you're the right person, the one we're looking for. The one Bird has been looking for. Right, Bird?"

Bird didn't say anything in response. Cooper was getting more and more confused. She'd be happy to play with the group. They sounded great, and the music was fantastic. But what was the big deal? They were acting as if she was auditioning to be the newest member of a superstar rock band.

"Bird?" Cooper said. "Are you okay?"

Bird smiled, looking more like the happy girl Cooper had first met. "Yeah," she said. "I was just thinking about the night I joined the group."

Someone giggled, then quieted down after a sharp look from Spider.

"Bird was the last person to join us," Spider said. Then he put his arm around Cooper's shoulder. "But perhaps you'll become the newest member. Are you ready for the trials to begin?"

Cooper stood with Spider's arm resting on her shoulders. The others were all watching her closely. She still wasn't sure what these so-called trials were all about, and part of her was a little suspicious. Then she thought about where she was and what was going on. It was a Midsummer gathering. All kinds of strange things were supposed to be happening. *This is probably just another one of the games*, she thought. *These guys are probably all part of some coven that plays at different festivals, and they're having a little fun with me.* Well, she could play games, too.

"Why not?" she said. "I have nothing else to do."

CHAPTER 4

Annie hurried down the path back to the cabin. She was annoyed at herself for leaving her paws behind. It meant she was missing out on all kinds of things. She wanted to start exploring the woods to see what kinds of surprises the different covens and other groups had set up in them. She'd already passed by some interesting-looking stuff, and she wanted to get a closer look. But she also wanted her costume to look perfect. She'd spent so much time on it, and she was proud of what she'd created. Several people had already commented on how great she looked. She couldn't wait to start walking around in full hedgehog gear so she could show off the whole outfit.

She came to the place where the main path broke off into smaller ones that led to the cabins. She knew that she, Cooper, and Kate had come down one of them on their way to the gathering, but now she couldn't recall which one it was. They all looked the same.

I should have left a trail of bread crumbs, she thought. *Like Hansel and Gretel did.*

She looked from one path to another. It was irritating how similar one narrow strip of dirt through the woods was to all the rest. Why didn't they have some kind of identifying markers? She was just going to have to pick one and see where it took her.

One of the paths led between two trees that sort of looked familiar to her. She decided to take that one, telling herself that she could always backtrack if it turned out not to be the correct way back to the cabin. Stepping onto it, she entered the forest.

It seems to be the right one, she thought as she walked. Because of the papier-mâché head, it was difficult to see much more than what was directly in front of her. But there was indeed something about the trees she was passing and the way the path twisted and turned that felt familiar to her. After a few minutes she stopped worrying and just enjoyed being in the woods. Pretty soon she would be at the cabin, and she could grab her paws and rejoin the others.

She couldn't help but wonder what kinds of surprises were in store for them. The dance later that night sounded like a lot of fun, but she was even more excited about the other things—the things no one had explained to her. She liked that everything had been kept a secret and that they would just have to wait and see what happened. It made the whole idea of Midsummer seem much more magical, like anything could happen and probably would.

She was thinking about this as the path took a turn and she found herself at a crossroads. One path went straight ahead while the other veered off to the right. She definitely didn't remember that from their walk earlier in the afternoon.

"Great," she said aloud. "Now what?"

She couldn't help but think about the last time she'd stood at a crossroads in the woods. It had been during the Tarot ritual they'd done in their Wicca study class just a couple of weeks ago. That night, wandering in the woods and meeting the coven members dressed up as various Tarot cards, she'd had an encounter with the goddess Hecate. Standing at the crossroads now, she wondered which path she should choose. Where did they each lead? Was one of them the path back to the cabin, or was she totally lost?

She couldn't decide. Perhaps one of them *was* the right path, but maybe they were both wrong. Maybe no matter which one she chose she would end up wandering around in the woods, lost, until she ran into someone or accidentally stumbled back onto the main road. It was probably best just to retrace her steps and start all over again, although that would mean losing a lot of time.

She sighed. Why did there have to be so many

paths? It was as if someone had deliberately wanted to confuse people who came into the woods. Plus, she realized that the hedgehog head was getting a little stuffy. Maybe she should take it off. After all, no one was around to see it anyway.

She started to lift the head from her shoulders when she heard a commotion in the woods. Someone was coming toward her down one of the paths. Whoever it was seemed to be rushing. Distracted, Annie left her head on and peered through the eyeholes to see who was coming.

It was a fox—not a real fox, but someone dressed as a fox. At first she thought it was the man she'd seen earlier at the opening circle. But as the figure came closer she saw that it was a different fox. This one was much more realistic than the other one had been. His mask seemed to be covered with real fur, and his tail was bushier. He seemed to be agitated about something and was looking around anxiously.

"There you are," he said as he rushed up to Annie, his whiskers quivering. He was panting, as if he'd been running for some time. "I've been looking for you."

"Me?" Annie said. "Why? Do I know you?"

"There's no time for games," the fox said. "It's growing late."

He stuck one of his paws into the pocket of his trousers and pulled something out. It looked like a letter.

"Here," he said, pressing it into Annie's hands. "Take it to the Oak King."

Annie looked at the letter, confused. "But what is it?" she asked.

"No time," the fox replied. "Take it to the Oak King. The hour is coming quickly."

"Time for what?" said Annie. "And who is the Oak King?"

"I knew they were foolish to trust this to a hedgehog," the fox said testily. "Silly creatures, all of you. Who is the Oak King? I don't have time for this, and neither do you. Now, go!"

He shooed Annie away with his paws, urging her down the second path. She danced away from him, the letter held tightly in her hand.

"But where is he?" she asked.

"That's for you to find out," the fox answered. "But hurry! Time is running out."

He turned and scampered back down the path he had come on, leaving Annie standing in the woods holding a piece of paper that looked a little worse for wear from having been in the fox's pocket. She stared at it stupidly. What was she supposed to do with it? He had told her to find the Oak King. But who was the Oak King, and where was she supposed to look for him? None of it made any sense.

She turned the letter over. The front was sealed shut with a large blob of green wax. In the center of the wax was an impression of what looked like holly leaves and berries. Annie was tempted to break the seal and read the contents of the letter. Maybe it would give her some clue as to what was going on. She ran her finger under the edge of the paper, preparing to open it, but something made her stop.

Maybe this is all part of the ritual, she thought. After all, the woman at the opening ceremony had told them to expect the unexpected. Maybe the Oak King was one of those surprises. The fox was likely a member of one of the participating covens, after all, and they had singled her out to take part in the festivities.

That put a new spin on things. It made her excited. She'd been chosen to play a role in part of the Midsummer celebration. And apparently it was an important part. The fox had said that she needed to find the Oak King right away because something was going to happen soon. She wondered what it was. Even more, she wondered where she would find this Oak King, whoever he was.

The fox had pointed her down the path she was on, so she decided she might as well keep walking on it. Probably the person playing the Oak King was waiting for her somewhere in the forest. She kept going, looking around for signs of someone who might provide the next clue.

She didn't see anyone for quite some time.

Then, as she was giving up hope, she found herself approaching an area where several large, open tents had been set up alongside the path. There were people going in and out of them.

"Excuse me," Annie said to a woman who had just stepped out of one of the tents. "Do you know where the Oak King is? I have a letter for him."

"So the messenger has been chosen," the woman said, smiling. "And a very interesting messenger indeed."

"So you know how I can find him?" Annie asked.

The woman nodded. "I can't tell you where he is," she said. "That would make your task too easy. But I can tell you this, he's not called the Oak King for nothing."

The woman disappeared back into the tent. Annie stood outside it for a moment, thinking about what she'd said. Why was the Oak King's name a clue? She had no idea. Why wouldn't anyone just come out and tell her where to go and what to do? Figuring out all of these puzzles was getting tiring. She decided to sit for a moment and think things through. Finding a large tree, she plopped down.

"Ow," she cried.

She'd sat on something hard. Reaching under herself, she pulled out an acorn and tossed it away. It landed a few feet from the tree, and she glared at it angrily. She'd been so excited over being chosen for one of the Midsummer games. Now she just felt frustrated.

She tried to force her mind to work. But for some reason her attention kept coming back to the acorn. Why? Then it hit her. Acorns. Oak trees.

"Of course!" she exclaimed. The Oak King would probably be found near the trees he was named for. She stood up, her enthusiasm renewed. Where would she find a lot of oak trees? In the woods, of course. But there were acres and acres of woods all around her. She didn't have time to search them all.

Some people were coming toward her on the path. They, too, were dressed in costumes, one of the men as Robin Hood and one of the women as Maid Marian. Annie rushed up to them.

"Is there an oak grove around here?" she asked. "Or maybe a really big oak tree?"

Robin looked at Marian and smiled, as if they were exchanging a secret. Marian nodded. Then Robin pointed down the path. "Go until the path starts to run uphill," he said. "Then leave it and walk to the left. You will see a yellow tent in the woods. Go there."

"Thanks," Annie said as she ran down the path.

She didn't want to waste any more time, and she went as quickly as she could. The path continued on without going either up or down, and she wondered if maybe Robin Hood had sent her on yet another wild-goose chase. But finally she felt herself starting to breathe more heavily, and she realized that the path was indeed beginning to slant upward.

She looked to her left. She didn't see any tent. Had she come far enough? Had she gone too far? She had no way of knowing, just as she had no way of knowing if Robin had told her the truth. But she also didn't have much choice, so, leaving the path, she began to wander through the trees.

After walking for a couple of minutes, she still hadn't seen any sign of a tent. She was hot and tired, and she was tempted to turn back. But then she reached the top of a little rise and stopped. She'd found the tent.

Sitting in the woods, pitched beneath a towering oak tree, was a large tent made of yellow silk. Ribbons of orange, red, and gold hung from the top and fluttered in the slight breeze. The colors reminded Annie of a tree in the fall, when all of its leaves turned from their summer colors to those of autumn. The tent's flaps were shut, so she approached and stood outside it.

"Hello?" she called. "I'm looking for the Oak King."

For a moment there was no answer. Then a voice said, "Enter."

Annie parted the opening of the tent and peered inside. There she saw a man sitting in a large wooden chair, almost like a throne. He was dressed in the same colors as the tent and its banners, his robe a deep yellow and the trim the various colors of fall leaves. He had a thick gray beard, although he didn't appear to be particularly old. On his head was a garland of leaves and acorns.

"Are you the Oak King?" Annie asked shyly. Although she knew the man was just someone playing a part, he still filled her with a sense of awe. He seemed so regal, and the way his eyes looked into her face made her feel like she should bow or something.

"I am the Oak King," the man replied. "Are you the messenger?"

Annie nodded. "I think so," she said. "Someone gave me this and told me to bring it to you."

She stepped forward and handed the Oak King the letter that was in her hand. The king took it and looked at it for a moment before slipping a finger beneath the folded paper and breaking the seal with a firm movement. He scanned the letter for a moment and then folded it again.

"So, we are to meet in his grove," he said. "Very well. You will accompany me, of course."

"Accompany you?" Annie repeated.

"To the meeting with my brother," the Oak King responded. "That is why you were chosen. A very good joke on my brother's part, choosing a hedgehog. He knows very well they sleep through winter.

Send one of my own creatures to invite me. I'll have to remember that when my turn comes. Perhaps I'll send a winter hare. That would put him in a fine mood."

"I don't understand," said Annie.

"I don't suppose you would," the king said. "Your kind do always become a little confused when the Midsummer magic is upon you. I daresay that's another reason my brother picked you. No matter. I'm sure you'll do just fine."

Annie didn't say anything. She was more confused than ever. She'd thought that her part in whatever was going on would end when she delivered the letter. Now, apparently, the Oak King expected her to go somewhere with him. She was sure that it was all part of the evening's festivities, but she would have liked a little more explanation.

"What do I have to do?" she asked.

The king waved a hand at her. "All in good time," he said. "It will be explained to you. For now, we must go. Night is coming, and I want to see what magic is taking place in the woods. By now Maeve should be about her business, and that is always something to look forward to."

"Maeve?" Annie said, testing out the sound of the strange name on her lips.

"Indeed," the Oak King replied. "The Faerie Queen herself. Have you not seen her?"

Annie shook her head.

"This is as much her night as it is my brother's and mine," said the king. "Those who meet her are lucky indeed—if they remember not to anger her."

"And what if they do?" Annie asked.

The king smiled. "Just hope you don't find out," he said, pushing open the tent flaps and stepping outside.

CHAPTER 5

The Faerie Queen looked down at Kate. She was much taller than Rowan. In fact, she didn't resemble Tyler's mother at all. But hadn't he said that his mother was playing the role of the queen? Or had she just assumed that? Suddenly, Kate couldn't remember much of anything. She was transfixed by the queen's face. Her dark eyes sparkled, and she wore a haughty expression that Kate thought was both proud and playful at the same time. She was dressed in gauzy robes of pink and purple that reminded Kate of the sky at twilight, and her black hair hung around her shoulders in waves. Slender wings, almost like those of a dragonfly, rose above her shoulders, and the fading sun shone through them like light through a stained-glass window.

"I am Maeve," the queen said. Once again her honeyed voice filled the air, reminding Kate of bees and flowers and long days spent doing nothing at all.

Maeve, Kate thought. It was an odd name, yet beautiful, too, much like the queen herself.

Kate thought about telling the queen that she was the Princess Goatcheese, but something told her that joking was not something Maeve would appreciate. "I'm Kate," she replied instead.

But the queen didn't seem to care what Kate's name was. She immediately asked her another question: "What are you doing in my woods?"

Kate was a little taken aback by Maeve's brusque attitude, but she answered politely. "I was talking to my boyfriend," she said.

The queen seemed more interested. "Boyfriend?" she said. "You mean your lover?"

Kate felt herself blushing. "Lover" seemed like such a strange thing for her to call Tyler. But was it so strange? Just a short time ago she had been thinking about telling him that she loved him. And wasn't that what a lover was—someone you were in love with? It might be an old-fashioned word, but she had to admit that it was accurate.

"Yes," she said. "I guess you could call him my lover."

"And where is your lover now?" asked Maeve.

"I don't know," Kate said truthfully. "He ran off." She didn't tell Maeve that Tyler had run off because of *her*. She didn't know why Tyler was so antsy about the queen when it clearly wasn't even his mother underneath the makeup and the costume, but she didn't want the woman playing the queen to think that she had somehow offended them.

"And what does he look like?" Maeve said, continuing her questioning.

"He's dressed as a raven," answered Kate. "With a mask of feathers."

This piece of information seemed to interest the queen greatly. She looked hard at Kate with an expression that was unreadable. *Whoever she is, she sure can act*, Kate thought to herself.

"You say your lover was costumed as a raven?" asked Maeve.

Kate nodded. "He's wearing all black. The mask is really great. You should see it."

Maeve ignored her. "Which way did he go?" she asked sharply.

Kate pointed down the path. "That way," she told the queen.

Maeve snapped her fingers. Suddenly two children—one a boy and one a girl—darted out from beneath her billowy skirts and stood beside her. Both had pale yellow hair the color of corn silk, and both had wings attached to the backs of the little blue tunics they were dressed in. They looked to Kate to be about eight or nine years old, and she wondered how they had managed to stay so quiet while tucked beneath the queen's gown.

Maeve leaned down and whispered something to the children. Almost immediately they ran into the trees, and once more Kate heard the laughter she had heard before the Faerie Queen's arrival. Was it coming from the children? Kate assumed that it was.

"Who were they?" she asked the queen. "They're really cute."

"My servants," Maeve answered. "Do not worry about them. Let us talk more about your lover."

"There's not much to talk about, really," said Kate. "I was just about to go look for him."

"A good idea," the queen said. "It is not wise to be apart from your lover on Midsummer Eve. He might find himself enchanted by another."

Kate couldn't help but think that Maeve looked at her strangely when she made the comment about Tyler's perhaps becoming enchanted by someone else. Was it some kind of reference to her own cheating? *That's ridiculous*, she told herself. *This woman couldn't possibly know about that.*

"Will you be at the dance later tonight?" Kate said quickly, not wanting to dwell too long on the issue of infidelity.

"You know about my dance?" asked Maeve, sounding surprised.

"Sure," said Kate. "Everybody does."

Maeve frowned. "I do not like mortals knowing my secrets," she said. "Did the raven tell you this?"

"No," Kate said. "Not exactly. The people organizing the ritual did."

The Faerie Queen looked at her intently. Kate looked away. She was feeling a little uncomfortable.

Why was Maeve acting so put out about the dance? Of course Kate would know about it. Was this just part of the queen's character? If so, what was Kate supposed to say?

"I don't think anyone meant to offend you," she said carefully. "We're all just very excited about Midsummer. Many people say it's their favorite night of the year."

Maeve gave her a little smile at hearing that. "As it is mine," she said. "So, you mortals have come here to celebrate my night? That explains why you are dressed like one of my people."

"Oh, yes," Kate answered, glad that Maeve seemed to be a little bit happier and thinking that perhaps she'd found the right thing to say. "And I hope my costume doesn't offend you. I thought it was appropriate for Midsummer, since this night is so special to you and all. In fact, we were hoping the faeries would come to the woods tonight. That's why we called you."

"Calling the faeries can be dangerous for mortals," the queen said. "Some would say it is a foolish thing to do."

"I don't think you could be dangerous," Kate said, getting into the game. "You're so beautiful."

"I can be very generous," Maeve told her. "To those I like, anyway. Others are not so fortunate. Tell me, girl, what is it that you most desire?"

Kate thought about the question. Since this was a game, she tried to think of what a girl in a fairy tale would say if she met the queen of the faeries in the woods. She thought about all of her favorite stories. In most of them the girls wanted to be beautiful or rich. But the one she'd always liked the best when she was little was "East of the Sun, West of the Moon." In that one a girl had to travel to the ends of the earth to find the prince she was in love with, after he'd been stolen away by evil trolls.

"True love," she said, not realizing at first that she had spoken aloud. But the more she thought about it, the more she realized that it really *was* the one thing she wanted most. She wanted to find Tyler, and she wanted him to know that he was the one she loved.

The queen of the faeries looked at Kate thoughtfully for a moment. She seemed to be thinking about something. Her eyes took on a peculiar shine, and she nodded to herself several times.

"Very well," she said finally. "Then true love it will be. But true love does not always come easily. You must go in search of it and pass my challenge."

Kate didn't understand. What was Maeve asking her to do?

"You want me to go find Tyler?" she said.

"I want you to search for the one who is your true love," the Faerie Queen said. "Whoever he might be."

That didn't seem like much of a challenge. All Kate had to do was track down her boyfriend and tell him that she loved him. She'd been hoping the

queen might suggest something a little more magical. But she didn't dare say anything. Whoever this
woman was, she seemed to be working really hard
at being the Faerie Queen, and Kate didn't want to
ruin the night for her by telling her that her suggestion was kind of lame.

"Sure," she said. "I'll go find him. Thanks for the
suggestion."

"It may not be as easy as you think, mortal girl,"
Maeve said. "Be sure you know your heart before
you choose."

Kate nodded. She noticed that it was beginning
to get darker, and she wanted to start looking for
Tyler before it became too dark to see anything. She
hadn't brought a flashlight, and the woods were
thick. Even with a strong moon, it would be difficult to see.

"Okay, then," she said to the queen. "'Bye.
Maybe I'll see you later at the dance."

"Perhaps you will," Maeve answered. "Good-bye
until then."

The queen turned and walked back into the
trees, her gown rustling softly as she moved. Kate
watched her go, then turned to continue down the
path. She wasn't sure where Tyler had run off to, but
that was the direction he'd been going in when
she'd last seen him, so it seemed like the logical
place to look.

The path went deeper into the woods. Here and
there Kate saw tents pitched among the trees and

people walking around. But none of them was a tall, thin guy dressed in black and wearing a feathered mask, so she kept walking. Tyler had to be around *somewhere*, and she was going to find him. Although the Faerie Queen's task for her wasn't as magical as she thought it could be, it was one she was anxious to complete.

As she walked farther and farther into the woods, the number of tents grew smaller. People seemed to want to stay as close to the main circle area as possible, and she guessed that now she was moving into a part of the forest that was too far away. Surely, Tyler hadn't gone that far, had he? He must have doubled back and returned to his campsite or to the main circle.

Irritated at having walked so far for nothing, Kate decided to go back herself. She was getting tired, it was getting dark, and she wasn't about to stumble around in the woods at night looking for Tyler, even if he was her boyfriend. She didn't know if he had planned the whole thing with the woman playing the Faerie Queen or not, but now she was annoyed at him for running off and leaving her alone.

Before she could turn around, though, she heard voices. They were coming from somewhere in front of her. Was it possible that there was a campsite ahead? Even if there was one, would Tyler be there? She had no reason to think that he would. She decided to forget about it.

Then she looked down and saw a black feather. It was lying at her feet, and she almost missed it in the gathering dusk. But there was no mistaking what it was when she held it up. It was shiny and black, just like the ones on Tyler's mask. He had come that way. Maybe it *was* him up ahead.

She walked toward the voices. The camp was only a few hundred feet ahead of her, tucked into a small clearing in the midst of some tall pines. As she approached, she saw that there were several tents set up and several people sitting around a fire in a stone circle.

She walked into the clearing, and the people around the fire looked up.

"What have we got here, boys?" said a guy's voice.

Kate groaned. She couldn't believe it. Evan Markson was sitting across the fire from her. He had a can of soda in one hand and a hot dog on a stick in the other, and he was grinning from ear to ear. *Just my luck*, Kate thought. *I come all the way out here and who do I run into but Scott's best friend.*

Then she noticed that the other guys gathered around the fire were also friends of Scott, either from the football team or from his after-school job. They were all staring at her, grinning like idiots, and she wanted to die. There she was, all dressed up like Princess Goatcheese the sugarplum fairy, and her ex-boyfriend's best friends were gawking at her like she was some kind of wacked-out window display.

"Nice outfit," one of them said, and the others laughed.

"For your information, I'm going to a costume party," Kate snapped. It was the only thing she could think of, and even as she said it she knew that they wouldn't buy it.

"In the middle of the woods?" Evan asked.

Kate decided that ignoring him was the best course of action. She couldn't tell them she was actually taking part in a Wiccan ritual, and there was really no other explanation for her costume or her appearance in the woods. "So, what are you guys doing here?" she countered.

Evan shrugged. "Same thing as you, I guess, only without the dress and wings."

Kate wanted to throw something at him. Evan had always been her least favorite of Scott's friends. He loved picking on her, and she knew that he wasn't real happy with her for breaking his best buddy's heart by dumping him. She wondered if Scott had told him about their kiss on the beach.

"Well, have a great time," she said sarcastically. "Try not to burn the forest down if you can help it. Remember, only you can prevent forest fires."

She started to leave, anxious to be away from the group of guys, but Evan called her back.

"Hang on," he said.

"What do you want?" asked Kate, folding her arms across her chest. She wasn't in the mood for any of Evan's teasing, and now it really was getting dark. She was far from the main camp, and she was angry. Why did these guys have to show up at what was supposed to be *her* Midsummer celebration? It wasn't that surprising, really. A lot of people camped in the woods. But why did they have to show up on this night of all nights?

"I have a surprise for you," Evan said. "Wait right here."

He stood up and darted into the trees. The other guys looked at Kate silently, some of them smiling. She was tempted to just leave, but she heard Evan coming back toward them.

"What is it?" said a voice in the trees. "I was looking for more wood."

Kate recognized that voice. She'd listened to it many times, dreamed about it even. When she heard it now, though, she really did almost turn and run as quickly as she could back into the forest. But it was too late. Evan emerged from the trees, dragging Scott behind him.

"See?" Evan said, pointing at Kate. "I told you you'd want to see this."

Scott looked at Kate, and his mouth dropped open. She was glad that it was almost dark so that he couldn't see how embarrassed she was. She wanted to kill Evan. How could he do this to her?

"Kate?" Scott said doubtfully. "Is that you?"

"Hey," Kate said weakly.

"What are you doing here?" Scott asked.

The guys were looking back and forth from Scott

to Kate, barely able to contain their glee. Evan in particular looked incredibly pleased with himself.

You jerk, Kate thought, glaring at him.

"I'm here with some friends," Kate told Scott. "You know, Annie and Cooper."

"You should have brought them along," one of the guys commented. "We could use some help with the cooking."

The rest of the guys laughed, but Scott didn't.

"You look nice," he said.

"Aww," Evan teased. "Isn't that romantic?"

Scott hit him in the arm. "Shut up, man. She does look nice."

"Thanks," Kate said. That was one thing she had always liked about Scott—he made her feel good about how she looked.

"Do you want to take a walk or something?" he asked, catching her off guard.

"I don't know," Kate answered. "I'm supposed to be getting back. I've got to meet the others soon. We're going to this costume party thing, and—"

"Can I walk you back at least?" he asked. "It's getting dark, and I have a flashlight."

Kate considered his offer. She knew it wasn't a good idea for her to go walking around in the woods with Scott. What if Cooper or Annie saw them? They were already giving her a hard enough time about him. Worse still, what if Tyler saw them? She hadn't told him about the kiss yet. If he saw her with Scott she would have even more explaining to do.

Then again, it *was* getting dark. She could really use some light to see her way by. And Tyler was the one who had led her on a wild-goose chase. It was his fault she was so far from the others. He really couldn't complain if she took Scott up on his offer to help. What if she just let Scott walk her part of the way back? She could leave him when she got to a familiar part of the forest, and no one would see them together. That didn't seem so bad.

"Okay," she said. "That would be nice."

CHAPTER 6

Who are these people? Cooper asked herself as she walked with Spider and the others through the woods. They said they weren't witches—or at least wouldn't say that they *were* witches—yet they had come to the Midsummer gathering. They were dressed in what looked like costumes, but at the same time Cooper could easily imagine them looking like this all of the time. They appeared to be normal teenagers, yet she couldn't help thinking that something wasn't quite *totally* normal about them. But when she tried to put her finger on exactly what it was, she couldn't. Like the songs they played, her thoughts about them moved too quickly to see clearly. She would think of something that seemed to explain how she felt about her new friends and then it would be gone, replaced by a thought about something completely different. It was as if someone were snatching away the pages of a story she was reading and substituting other pages, from a different story, for them.

She was walking beside Spider. The boy moved quickly through the woods. He clearly knew his way through the maze of paths that crisscrossed the forest, barely pausing when they came to a place where a decision had to be made about which direction to go in. But where were they going? Did they have a cabin or a campsite somewhere? No one had told Cooper anything—they'd just started walking. All she knew was that she was on her way to some kind of trial. But what was that supposed to mean? She still had no idea what it would entail, but she figured she would go along with it. Spider and the others seemed okay, and she really liked their music. If going through with their little games meant that she got to play with them some more, she was glad to do it.

This in itself puzzled her a little bit. Normally, she didn't care what other people thought about her. She had never been one to try to ingratiate herself into a group. Why did she care now? She told herself that it was because of the music. It had gotten inside her head and was haunting her like a lovely, ghostly voice. She still heard snatches of it from time to time, and she longed to hear it and to play it again.

"Where do you all live?" Cooper asked Spider, tired of walking in silence.

"We live close to here," Spider said. "But most people never visit our home."

"Why?" asked Cooper.

"Maybe they're afraid that they'll like it and

won't want to leave," Spider said.

Cooper didn't understand. Spider never answered questions directly. It was like he was hiding something. *I guess it doesn't matter*, Cooper told herself. If they wanted to be all mysterious, that was fine with her. She didn't like it when people asked her a lot of questions either.

But there were some questions that she did want answers to, starting with whether or not Spider really knew where he was going or if he was just trying to show off. Cooper was happy to walk around in the woods, even at night, but she wasn't keen on the idea of getting completely lost. Spider seemed to be taking them straight into the middle of nowhere. He'd even left the path and begun to weave among the trees in an apparently random way.

"Are you sure you know where we're headed?" Cooper asked.

Spider stopped. "Are you doubting me?" he asked, sounding a little annoyed.

"I'm just wondering where we're going," Cooper explained. "These woods are huge, and it's easy to get lost."

Spider laughed, but the others remained silent. "I could never get lost in the woods," Spider said. "Trust me."

He turned and continued to walk without saying anything else about the matter. The others followed obediently, and a moment later Cooper joined them. Spider did seem sure of himself, and

Cooper respected that. Spider reminded her a lot of herself—headstrong and confident. It couldn't hurt to go along with him.

They were walking downhill now, passing between two rows of trees whose branches formed a sort of tunnel above them. At the end of it another hill rose up in the shadows, and Spider stopped at the foot of the hills.

"This is the place of testing," he said.

Cooper looked around. There didn't seem to be anything there except the woods and the hills. What kind of a test were they going to do? A line of rocks ringed the bottom of the hills, but there wasn't anything particularly interesting about them.

Then Spider pointed to a dark space between two of the rocks. "In there is a cave," he said. "We call it the Cave of Vision."

"Uh-huh," Cooper said, eyeing the entrance to the cave warily. "You go inside there?"

"Yes," Spider replied in a tone that Cooper found almost mocking.

"And what do you do in there?" asked Cooper.

"Why don't you tell her, Bird?" Spider answered.

Bird hadn't said a word during the entire walk. Now she stood nervously beside Cooper. "It is a place of seeing," she explained. "A place of great power."

"The shamans of old knew the power of the

caves," Spider added. "They came here to perform their rituals."

"What kind of rituals?" Cooper asked.

"I cannot tell you that until you agree to enter the cave," Spider responded. "Do you agree?"

Cooper hesitated. Going into a cave in the middle of the woods seemed like a really good way to get into trouble. Caves weren't normally empty—things usually lived in them. Things like bats and bears and other creatures that wouldn't take kindly to being disturbed. What if she crawled in there and came face-to-face with a grizzly that was thinking about dinner?

"Do you guys really know what you're doing?" she asked. "I mean, this sounds like fun and all, but if you're just doing this because it's Midsummer and we're all supposed to be getting into magic and whatever, then don't do it on my account. I'm perfectly happy to just hang out and play music if you want to."

"I think perhaps you made a mistake in choosing this one," Spider said to Bird. "I don't think she's ready for us."

"No," Bird said, sounding anxious. "She came to me. She's the one."

Bird turned to Cooper. "Please," she said. "You heard the music. You felt it. Don't you want to play with them?"

Cooper looked at the other girl's face. She seemed so upset. But why? Why was it so important to her that Cooper play with Spider and the others? Sure, the music had been great, but Cooper wasn't about to do something stupid just because these kids wanted to play a game.

Bird took her hand. "Please, Cooper," she said. "It's important."

Cooper sighed. Bird seemed like a nice girl. Cooper still wasn't sure what all of this was about, but she was starting to suspect that it was all part of the overall ritual. She thought back to the night of her Wicca dedication ceremony. They'd been told that there would be different tests throughout their year and a day of study. Maybe this was one of them. Cooper wouldn't put it past Sophia and Archer and the rest of the teachers in their weekly study group to plan something like this. After all, they'd done equally strange things before, like dressing up as Tarot cards and having the class members talk to them. Why not do something like this? Maybe one of them was even waiting inside the cave to surprise Cooper.

"Okay," she said. "But are you sure there are no bears in there?"

Bird's face relaxed into a shy smile. "No bears," she said. "Come on."

She took Cooper's hand and led her to the opening in the rocks. It hardly looked big enough to squeeze through, but as Cooper watched, Bird ducked into the space and disappeared. A moment later her hand emerged, beckoning to Cooper.

Cooper stepped into the tiny space. She was sure she would get stuck, but after sticking her head through she saw that it opened up almost immediately. She slid her body in as if slipping through the crack of a partially closed door. Then she was in the cave, standing next to Bird.

She was surprised at how large the cave was and how light it was inside. Outside, the sun had been rapidly fading into darkness, and she'd expected it to be totally black inside the cave. But the space was filled with a soft luminescence that came from somewhere up above. Was it possible that there were lights in the cave? Cooper doubted it, but she didn't see any openings in the cave's ceiling that explained the pale green glow.

The space itself was about twenty feet in diameter, with smooth rock walls and a stone floor. It was as if someone had completely hollowed out the hill and left only the shell. In the center of the floor there was a circle of stones.

"This cave has been here for centuries," Bird explained as Spider entered the cave behind them.

"How did you find it?" asked Cooper, amazed. The cave was incredible. She'd never seen anything like it, and she couldn't believe that something like it existed practically in her backyard.

"These woods have long been known to us," Spider said, overhearing Cooper's question.

He talks like he's three hundred years old or something, Cooper thought. Someone in one of the covens must have known about the cave and decided to use it in the Midsummer celebration. She wondered what other surprises there were in the woods. Were Annie and Kate having equally interesting experiences, or were they just wandering around looking for her? She hoped not. She wanted to think that they were having adventures of their own.

Bird led Cooper over to the circle of stones in the middle of the floor and motioned for her to sit. Now that Cooper was inside the cave and saw that it wasn't a damp, nasty place, she was getting into things, and she couldn't wait to see what came next. She thought Bird would sit beside her, but the girl said, "I must leave you now. But I will be waiting for you if—when—you return from your journey."

"What do you mean?" Cooper said, confused. "You're not staying? What about the others?"

"This testing is for you alone," Bird said. "Spider will guide you."

Before Cooper could protest, Bird slipped through the entrance, leaving Cooper alone in the cave with Spider. A moment later Spider emerged from the back of the cave carrying an armload of sticks, which he arranged in the ring of stones. Then he struck something against one of the stones, sending sparks into the air.

It's a fire pit, Cooper thought as the sticks began to burn brightly. She wondered where the smoke would go, but it streamed toward the ceiling and disappeared, so she assumed there was some kind of vent up there.

Spider sat down directly across the fire from Cooper.

"You have accepted the challenge," he said. "It is time for the dreaming to begin." His voice had taken on a tone that Cooper hadn't heard before. It sounded like the voice of someone who had done this many times, who was used to leading others. Spider suddenly seemed very old to Cooper. *But he can't be much older than I am*, she thought. Was he really going to lead a ritual? Well, why not? Cooper, Annie, and Kate did rituals on their own. And Tyler, who was their age, often took part in his coven's rituals. Maybe Spider really *was* a witch and was just putting on an act to get Cooper more into what was happening.

Spider opened a small pouch painted with symbols and decorated with feathers. He poured something that looked like sand into his outstretched palm and then tossed it onto the fire. A huge cloud of purplish smoke rose from the circle of stones, and for a few moments the flames themselves took on a purple color before returning to their usual orange and yellow.

The smoke, however, did not disappear. It hovered around them like a fog. Cooper thought she also detected the smell of flowers. She was surprised that the smoke wasn't causing her to choke or making it difficult for her to breathe. But it just floated in the air, swirling around as if someone was stirring it with an invisible stick.

"Close your eyes," Spider instructed her.

Cooper let her eyelids fall shut. The smell of the purple smoke was growing stronger, and that, combined with the warmth of the cave, was making her a little drowsy. She feared she might fall asleep, so she tried hard to concentrate on what Spider was saying.

"We have entered the Cave of Vision," Spider said. "It is a doorway to another place, a place some of us know well but which you have never before entered. Tonight we will journey to that place. It will not be easy. There will be tests. Whether you succeed or fail depends on how well you perform these tests. Are you ready to begin?"

Cooper took a deep breath. She assumed that Spider was going to lead her on some kind of guided meditation. How hard could that be? She'd done guided meditations dozens of times. All she had to do was follow the words of the leader. Was that the big challenge Spider had been talking about? If so, she was sure she could handle it.

"Yes," she said. "I'm ready."

A moment later she felt the air around her change again. Spider had thrown something else on the fire, and the smell of flowers grew stronger.

Cooper breathed it in, feeling it fill her head. It also made her more relaxed, almost as if she were drifting into that fuzzy state that occurred between waking and sleeping. *I can't fall asleep*, she thought dreamily.

"You are walking down a path," Spider said. "You have journeyed far, and you have a long way still to go."

Cooper imagined herself walking on a path. That was easy. Then, out of nowhere, she felt someone take her hand. The sudden touch startled her, and she opened her eyes. Spider was standing beside her, the purple smoke blowing around him.

"Come with me," he said.

Cooper stood up. She was confused. Where were they going to go? Wasn't this supposed to be a meditation? What was he doing?

Spider led her through the smoke in the direction of the rear of the cave. Was there something back there? Cooper's head swam, and she wanted to sit down. There was something strange about the smoke. She felt like she was dreaming, but she knew she wasn't. She could feel the cave floor beneath her feet, and she could smell the smoke and feel Spider's fingers around hers.

"Where are you taking me?" she asked him.

"To the doorway," he answered. "It's where the path leads you."

Cooper expected to find a solid wall at the back of the cave. But as Spider led her to what she suspected was the farthest part of the cave she saw that a tunnel passed into the stone. Spider led her into it.

"I hope this leads out of here," Cooper said, noting that the ceiling of the tunnel seemed to be getting lower as they walked. "I think I need some fresh air."

"In a moment," Spider said. "First you must pass through the doorway."

Cooper was about to ask what this doorway was that Spider kept talking about, but before she could she found out for herself as they came to an opening in the tunnel. Something was covering it, so she couldn't see what lay beyond, but she could feel a breeze coming through so she knew that they couldn't be too far away from the outside.

Spider stopped. "By entering the Cave of Vision and passing through it you have come to the doorway between the world of men and the world of Faerie," he said solemnly. "Should you choose to pass through this doorway you will be entering a realm of magic. I cannot tell you what will happen there. Are you ready to risk this?"

Cooper nodded. "Sure," she said, figuring that anything would be worth agreeing to if she could just get outside again and into the fresh air.

Spider nodded. "Very well," he said. "Then you may pass through. On the other side there will be someone to greet you and act as your guide in the

Faerie realm. Your testing has begun."

A guide, Cooper thought. They were really going all out with their little game. Who was this going to be?

Spider stepped forward and swept aside whatever was covering the opening of the tunnel. Beyond it, Cooper could see shadows and moonlight.

"You may enter," Spider said.

Cooper stepped out of the tunnel. Immediately the opening was closed up again, and she was standing by herself in the woods. *I must be on the other side of the hill*, she thought, looking around. But there was no one there to meet her, no guide as Spider had promised.

Then someone stepped from the shadows. Cooper gave a start when she saw who—or what—it was. It seemed to be human, but it was covered in leaves and dirt. It looked like one of the boys from Spider's group, but even wilder.

"Who are you?" she asked. "And what are we supposed to do now?"

The boy cocked his head to one side and stared at her, but didn't say anything.

"What's your name?" Cooper tried, but the boy just scuttled away from her and stared some more.

He's acting like a wild animal, Cooper thought with annoyance. Fine, if that was the way he wanted to be, she could play the game, too.

"Okay, Wild Man," she said, coming up with a

name for her new companion. "You're supposed to lead me on the next part of this trip. So lead on."

The Wild Man looked at her for another moment. Then he turned and walked into the trees. *I guess I said the right thing*, Cooper thought, and hurried after him.

CHAPTER 7

"But I have to get the rest of my costume and get back to my friends," Annie protested, following the Oak King out of the tent.

The king ignored her, striding into the woods. She scrambled to keep up. She really wanted to get back to the cabin to find her paws, but she felt as if she'd sort of agreed to take part in whatever it was the Oak King was doing. If it was part of the Midsummer ritual—and she was sure that it was—she couldn't just quit. If she'd been selected to play a role in the celebration, she had to see it through.

Okay, she told herself. *For right now you're a hedgehog helping the Oak King. What would you do?*

She had no idea. She didn't even know who the Oak King was, where they were going, or what was expected of her. All she knew was that she was supposed to follow him. And that's what she did. As the king made his way through the woods, she tried to stay right with him. Although he didn't seem to be rushing, he walked quickly, and she had a hard time keeping up.

"It's just like him to pick an inconvenient spot," the king said irritably. Annie wasn't sure if he was speaking to her or to himself, so she didn't say anything.

"At least it gives me a chance to see the woods," continued the Oak King. "It's always at its best on Midsummer, although of course Yule is wonderful, too. Still, summer has a life to it that winter doesn't. I'll give it that much. But that's as much Maeve's doing as it is his." He turned to Annie. "Although he'll want you to believe that it's all *his* work, you know."

"You mean your brother?" asked Annie.

The Oak King nodded. "That's right," he said. "Arrogant fellow."

"It doesn't sound like you two get along very well," Annie commented.

The Oak King laughed. "Oh, we get along well enough," he said. "You know how it is with brothers—fight one day, make up the next. Have you any siblings?"

"One," said Annie. "A sister. Meg."

"And do the two of you fight often?" the king asked.

Annie shook her head. "Not so much," she said. "But when we do it's usually a big one."

"That's what I mean," said the king. "My brother and I fight like anything. Of course, it's only twice a year, and that's probably less than most."

"Only twice a year?" Annie said, puzzled. "It sounds like you schedule them."

"We do," said the king. "Midsummer and Yule. Every year."

It seemed odd to Annie that the Oak King and his brother fought on set days. When she and Meg fought it was almost always because one of them had flown off the handle for no real reason. The last time they'd fought had been when Meg had accidentally spilled a glass of milk all over the paper Annie had just spent four hours writing for English class. Annie had reacted hastily, and Meg had run away in tears. But they'd made up quickly.

"What do the two of you fight about?" Annie asked.

The Oak King sighed. "That's a long story," he said, "and best left for later. Why don't you tell me something about yourself first."

"Like what?" Annie asked. She couldn't really think of anything to tell the Oak King that would be interesting.

"What about your family," the king said. "Apart from your sister, I mean. Tell me about them."

"I live with my aunt," replied Annie. "She's great. We get along really well."

"And your parents?" asked the king. "What about them?"

Annie felt herself tense up. She didn't like to answer questions about her parents. Normally, she avoided talking about them with anyone but her closest friends, and even they didn't know all that much.

Her companion sensed her hesitation and stopped walking. He turned and looked at Annie, who was trying to think of something to say to change the subject. But the king wouldn't have it.

"Come, hedgehog," he said. "What of your family? Surely you have a mother and a father?"

Annie cleared her throat. "Yes," she said reluctantly, "I do have a mother and a father. Or I did once."

"Once?" said the Oak King. "Meaning you don't now?"

"No," said Annie. "They're dead."

"How?" the king asked immediately.

Annie was taken aback. Usually when she said that her parents were dead people started apologizing all over themselves, as if she was the one who was dying and they'd somehow offended her. But the king simply stared at her expectantly, waiting for an answer.

She wasn't sure how to reply. Who was this man asking such personal questions? He didn't even know her. She didn't have to tell him anything she didn't want to. But she was surprised to find that another part of her wanted to tell him. For reasons she couldn't understand, she liked him. She didn't know anything about him, yet she felt close to him.

"It was a long time ago," she said finally.

The king gazed at her silently. She knew he was waiting for her to tell him her story. But she just couldn't. As much as she liked him she couldn't talk about that. This was Midsummer. It was supposed to be a happy time. She didn't want to spoil that.

"I think now I must continue on my way," the Oak King said after a moment. "The time for meeting my brother is not far off, and I have much to do before then."

He began walking again.

"Wait," Annie called out. "Don't you still need me?" She had thought that she was supposed to be traveling with the king wherever he was going.

"I'm not sure that you will want to be part of this," the king said, sounding serious. "I think perhaps your journey with me has ended."

"But why?" Annie asked. "I thought you needed my help."

The king sighed. "My way is difficult," he said. "You are tired. Perhaps you have done enough for this Midsummer night."

"But I want to help you," Annie insisted. She didn't understand why he suddenly didn't want her along. He had seemed so insistent before that she accompany him. Was he angry because she wouldn't answer his questions about her parents? She was afraid she'd disappointed him somehow.

The Oak King looked at her face for some time without speaking. His eyes seemed incredibly sad to Annie. Then he nodded.

"Perhaps you need to come with me after all," he said. "Perhaps you will be ready when the time comes."

"Ready for what?" Annie asked. She was pleased that the king was going to let her accompany him, but she still didn't know what they were going to do. "Time for what?" she asked, trying again.

But the Oak King was already walking away.

As she followed the Oak King through the forest, Annie hoped that he would tell her more about what they were doing, but he didn't. She wondered what could be awaiting them when they reached wherever it was they were going. The king had said that she might not be ready for it, whatever it was, but she couldn't imagine what he was talking about.

The Oak King didn't talk very much as they walked, only pausing occasionally to point out various things to her like the calls of birds or the fleeting shadow of a deer or rabbit running into the trees. Annie was amazed at how much he saw that she didn't, how connected he seemed to be to the world of the woods. It was as if he was as much a part of them as the trees and animals themselves.

They'd gone quite a way without seeing any other people when suddenly Annie heard voices ahead. It sounded like many people enjoying themselves. Hearing them, the Oak King stopped.

"It seems we are here," he said. "Come, little hedgehog. It is time for it to begin."

Finally, Annie thought. *Now I'll find out what this is all about.*

They walked into a large clearing and found themselves in the middle of what seemed to be a party. Torches were lit all around the glade, illuminating a long table piled with food and drink. People in fantastic costumes were gathered around it, talking and laughing. When they saw the Oak King and Annie they cheered joyfully.

"At last you are here," said a man who jumped up and ran over to embrace the Oak King. Annie saw that it was the man dressed as Robin Hood, the very one she'd met earlier on the path.

"I see you found what you were searching for," he said to her.

Annie smiled inside her mask. Robin was clearly having a good time, as was everyone else at the table. She didn't see anything about the party that would be unpleasant, and she wondered again why the Oak King had suggested she remain behind. Didn't he want her to have fun on her first Midsummer celebration?

"Come, my lord," said Robin, putting his arm through the king's and leading him to the table. "We've set a place for you at the head."

The Oak King settled into a large chair at one end of the table. Robin motioned for Annie to take a seat beside him and Maid Marian, and she did. Then Robin lifted his glass.

"A toast," he said. "To our once and future king."

The people around the table raised their glasses and cheered. "To the king!" some said, while others simply added "Hurrah" and "Likewise." Annie raised the goblet in front of her. She had to remove her mask in order to drink, and as she took it off she saw people stealing glances at her, as if they'd been waiting to see what she looked like beneath the hedgehog head. Ignoring them, she took a sip from her glass, raising the edge of her mask to reach her mouth.

"What is this?" she asked. The drink was sweet and thick, and she'd never tasted anything like it.

"It's mead," Maid Marian informed her. "Made from honey and who knows what. The boys spend all week making it."

"It's good," Annie said, taking another sip.

She realized suddenly that she was famished. She hadn't eaten anything since the sandwich at the cabin several hours before, and her stomach began to growl as she smelled all of the food on the table. There was fresh baked bread and roasted chicken, platters of fruit and hunks of cheese. It looked like one of the spreads Kate's caterer mother would make, and Annie was dying to eat some of it.

"You all look as if you need a little something," the Oak King said from his place at the head of the table, as if reading her thoughts. "Eat. The night is fleeting, and there is much to come."

All around the table, people piled their plates with food. Annie did the same, biting eagerly into a piece of chicken. It was delicious, and she ate steadily for some time before she felt satisfied enough to slow down. Then she turned to Maid Marian and Robin, who were sharing a sliced apple.

"This is some party," she said. "Do you always do this on Midsummer?"

Robin nodded. "It's our tradition," he said. "Do you not do the same?"

"This is all new to me," Annie told him. "I haven't been practicing very long."

"The people of the wood have gathered like this since time immemorial," Maid Marian said.

"The king said that something was going to happen later," said Annie. "What was he talking about?"

"The battle, of course," answered Robin, draining his cup of mead and refilling it.

"With his brother?" Annie asked.

"Yes," said Robin. "They fight on this night every year."

"He mentioned that," Annie responded. "I didn't realize they had a party first."

Marian glanced at Robin. "Perhaps, as she is new, she doesn't know about the ritual," she said.

Robin nodded. "Let me explain," he said. "Tonight the Oak King will battle his brother, the Holly King. We are here to help him prepare."

The Holly King, Annie thought. *So that's his name.* It made sense that the Oak King's brother was also a king, but she wondered what he was the king of. For that matter, what was the Oak King the king of? She didn't know that either. "What are they fighting about?" she wondered aloud.

"The kingship of the wood," said Marian.

"And of the year," added Robin.

"Of the year?" repeated Annie, not understanding.

"Each Midsummer and Yule the brothers meet and fight to see who will rule for the next six months," Robin explained. "They come together and fight to the death."

"To the death!" said Annie, startled.

"Of course," said Robin, as if it should be obvious to anyone. "The winner reigns for the next six months, and then they battle again."

Annie was about to ask how they could possibly do battle again when one of them was dead. Then she remembered that it was all a game, an elaborate ritual that she had become caught up in. Of course, nobody really died. They just acted out the battle. It was like the Renaissance fair she had gone to the previous summer, where everyone had worn medieval costumes and pretended to be knights and ladies. Only this time the players were acting out some kind of pagan ritual she'd never heard of.

"I wonder who will win," she said, getting into the spirit of things. "I hope it's the Oak King."

"Oh, no," Marian said. "It will be the Holly King."

"How do you know already?" said Annie.

"Because that's the way it always is," Robin told her.

Annie was puzzled. What fun was the mock battle if everyone already knew how it ended? It seemed to her that it should be left up to chance. If the Oak King always lost and the Holly King always won, why even bother?

"Maybe this time it will be different," she said hopefully.

Marian and Robin looked at her kindly and didn't say anything. At the other end of the table, the Oak King stood up and clapped his hands. "It's time for the entertainment," he called out. "What have you prepared for me this year?"

There was a lot of commotion as people jumped up and ran around. Annie sat, watching and waiting to see what was going to happen next. She was really enjoying the evening so far, and she was anxious to see more. Even the battle sounded like fun now that she sort of understood what it was about.

A man walked into the center of the clearing. He was dressed in white and green, and when he appeared everyone began to boo loudly. Annie wondered why they didn't like the man, but then she realized that they were just pretending to dislike him. It was like the hissing people did when a villain appeared on stage. The man stood, tapping his foot impatiently, until the noise died down.

"I am Winter," he said pompously, bringing more boos from the audience.

"I am Winter," he said again, more loudly than the first time. "And this is my poem." He cleared his throat and recited.

> As the year begins to wither,
> and the sun burns out his days,
> I, the Holly King, grow stronger,
> and await my time to reign.
> On Midsummer eve I come
> to best my brother in fair fight,
> soon the wood will wear my mantle,
> cold as ice and snowy white.
> Are you ready, my dear brother?
> Will you join me on the field?
> We all know how it will end—
> that to my mighty sword you'll yield.

The man stopped, and the clearing filled with more boos and hisses. The speaker seemed to be waiting for something, looking around haughtily at the spectators.

Then someone else ran into the clearing. It was a man dressed all in bright yellow and orange. Long triangles of different warm colors spoked out from his back, and he resembled a huge shining sun. When the man in green saw him he jumped back as if frightened. The yellow man stopped in front of him and pointed a finger at him as he began to recite his own poem.

> Fight I will, oh frozen creature!
> Ice and snow I do not fear.
> While your time may soon be coming,
> I still have some hours here.
> On this field we will battle,
> and you may emerge the king.
> But in six months I'll return
> to end your frigid reign with spring.
> So do your best, my wintry brother.
> Swing your sword and take your aim.
> Your time, too, will soon be over,
> and my light will shine again.

As he finished, the man in yellow lunged at the man in green, who began running wildly around the clearing with the yellow man in pursuit. The crowd around the table hooted and shrieked in merriment, watching their comical actions, and Annie found herself laughing so hard she could hardly breathe. When she looked up she saw that the Oak King, too, was laughing loudly.

"Very good!" he cried. "Very good indeed! Much improved upon last year. My blessings on you both."

The two men paused in their chase to bow briefly to the Oak King. Then the man in green darted into the trees with the man in yellow on his heels. When they were gone a group of people with instruments replaced them and immediately began to play a song. A woman stepped forward and began to sing.

> *Summer fades like dreams unwinding,*
> *days grow shorter, nights grow long.*
> *Now the Oak King passes over,*
> *goes to sleep to be made strong.*
> *When the sun is born again we'll*
> *greet him on the darkest night.*
> *Then he comes with blazing glory,*
> *bringing back the warmth and light.*

Unlike the comic poems of the first two performers, the woman's song made Annie feel sad. She was singing about the beauty of summer fading, when it seemed as if summer had just begun. Why was everyone talking about such depressing things? She thought that Midsummer was supposed to be a happy time, a time of magic and fun. They were making it into something else. She didn't want to think about death. It made her think of her parents, and she'd done enough of that for one night. Now she wanted to dance and sing. She hoped the midnight dance with her friends was going to be more like that.

Everyone else seemed to like the song, though.

When the players started to play it again, everyone joined in, their voices filled with sadness as they sang about the death of the Oak King. But as Annie listened she realized that there was hopefulness in the song, too. They talked of his coming back and bringing the light with him. That was a nice image. But it still made her sad to think about his dying, so she was glad when the song ended and the Oak King stood up.

"It is almost time," he said. "Now I must go prepare myself for battle. Will those helping me please attend?"

Robin Hood stood up. He tapped Annie on the shoulder. "We must go help him," he said to her.

"Me?" Annie said.

Robin nodded. "Of course," he said. "You have been his squire all evening. You're expected to continue to be so now."

CHAPTER 8

"So you're here with Annie and Cooper?" Scott asked Kate. They'd been walking for almost ten minutes in silence, neither knowing what to say.

"Yeah," Kate replied. "And some other friends, too. It's kind of a party. A costume party."

"I didn't think that was your usual camping gear," Scott joked.

The flashlight cast a long, thin beam of light out ahead of them. That light, added to the moonlight that slipped through the arms of the trees, meant that it really wasn't terribly dark in the woods. Kate was surprised at how well she could actually see. The moon was only about halfway to fullness, but the strength of its light was unusual. The moonshine almost seemed to glow, covering the trees and the forest floor in an unearthly silver skin. It had a magical quality to it that made her both excited and a little nervous. It was as if someone had spilled faerie dust over the whole forest.

Thinking of that reminded her of the Faerie Queen. Kate wondered where she was now. Was she back in the main clearing, preparing for the dance? Was she in another part of the woods, giving someone else a challenge for the night? Whoever had organized things had gone to a lot of trouble to make the experience a fun one. Kate hoped Annie and Cooper were having a good time, wherever they were.

"I've been meaning to call you," Scott said, interrupting her thoughts.

Kate didn't respond. She was beginning to think that letting Scott escort her back had been a bad idea. There were a lot of things between them that hadn't been resolved, and she wasn't sure she was really up for talking about any of them.

"About what happened at Skip Day—" Scott began.

"I'm sorry about that," said Kate quickly, cutting him off and hoping he would let the subject drop.

"I'm not," Scott told her. "Why are you?"

Kate sighed. "It just shouldn't have happened," she replied. "We're not together anymore, remember?"

"That wasn't my idea," said Scott in a wounded tone. "It was yours. And you never really told me why you were breaking up with me anyway."

Now Kate was sure that walking back with him had been one of her stupider decisions. Had she really expected him not to say anything about the kiss or about their breakup?

"It just wasn't going to work out," she tried.

"How do you know?" asked Scott, sounding a little angry. "You didn't even give it a chance. I turned down a full scholarship so that we could find out, but you just gave up without even trying."

"I didn't just give up," Kate answered defensively.

"But you can't tell me why you think it wouldn't work," said Scott.

It wasn't that Kate couldn't tell him because she didn't know. It was that she couldn't tell him because she wasn't ready for him to know the truth. When it came down to it, she'd gotten Scott in the first place because she'd put a spell on him. Even though he'd stuck around after she and her friends had taken the spell back, the fact was that she could never be entirely sure why he wanted to be with her. There was always that little doubt in her mind that if she hadn't worked magic on the doll that resembled him he would never have asked her to the Valentine's Day dance and they would never have gotten together.

More important, there was no way she could ever tell him about her interest in witchcraft. He just wouldn't understand that. But Tyler could understand it. He *did* understand it, because he was a witch himself. She didn't have to hide who she was from him like she did from Scott. She didn't have to worry that Tyler would make fun of her or think that she was weird because she liked to do rituals and work magic.

But you never gave Scott a chance to find out how he would react, a voice in her head reminded her. *You just assumed he wouldn't be able to handle it.*

She didn't want to think about that. It was true, she never had given Scott a chance to react to the news that she was studying Wicca. But she didn't think she had to. He just wasn't the kind of guy who would understand what it was all about. He understood football strategy and cars and stuff like that. He didn't really think about things a lot the way she did—and the way Tyler did.

"I thought we had something really special, Kate," Scott said softly, interrupting her thoughts. "I don't know what I did wrong. Was it because I broke up with you first? Was that it? I told you why I did that."

"No," Kate said. "It had nothing to do with that."

"Then why won't you tell me what it was?" he said, sounding more and more frustrated. "Was it that other guy?"

Kate's heart jumped in her chest. "What other guy?" she asked.

"I don't know his name," Scott said. "Some tall guy with black hair. Kind of thin. I saw you walking downtown with him one night. I was going to say hello, but you looked like you were having a good time so I didn't."

Tyler. Scott had seen her with Tyler. Kate didn't know why that made her feel bad, but it did. She'd been careful not to go places where too many people could see them. But they did go out to movies occasionally, and sometimes for dinner, so it wasn't really a shock that Scott had seen them together.

"Is he your boyfriend?" asked Scott. "Is he the reason you broke up with me?"

Kate found herself unable to speak. Yes, Tyler was the reason she'd broken up with Scott. Yes, he was her boyfriend. But hearing Scott say it that way—as if the very thought that it might be true wounded him deeply—made it sound as if she'd been having an affair or something. It wasn't like that at all. Or was it? After all, she *had* kissed Tyler only minutes after telling him that she had another boyfriend. Now she was all confused. She'd wanted the break between her and Scott to be a clean one, but now it was turning into something complicated.

"Tyler is a nice guy," she said, knowing it was the wrong thing to say.

"So you *are* dating him?" Scott said, sounding both sad and angry.

"I guess so," Kate answered, immediately feeling guilty about not being entirely truthful, both to Scott and to Tyler. "I mean yes, we're going out."

"Why couldn't you just tell me that?" said Scott.

"It wasn't that simple," Kate responded. "I didn't break up with you because of Tyler. He was just the thing that made me see that I had to."

"That makes a lot of sense," said Scott sarcastically. "He's not the reason you dumped me, but he made you see that you had to, and now you're dating him. It sure sounds to me like he's the reason."

Kate wanted to be angry at Scott, but she couldn't. He was right. She wasn't making any sense. She tried to see things from his perspective, and when she did she saw how ridiculous what she was saying must sound. She searched for words that would help him understand, but she couldn't find them.

Scott stopped walking. Kate kept going, but Scott grabbed her hand and pulled her back. She refused to look at him.

"Kate, I really want to be with you," he said. "You're not like any girl I've ever been out with. You're smart, and funny, and really beautiful."

Kate could feel herself starting to cry. She didn't want Scott to be nice to her. She wanted him to be angry. That would make things so much easier. This way he was forcing her to think about things she didn't want to think about.

"Don't you remember how much fun we had?" he continued. "Don't you miss that?"

"Scott, I have to go," Kate said.

"Why?" said Scott. "Do you have to meet Tyler?"

Part of Kate wanted to defend her boyfriend, but another part of her didn't want to hurt Scott any more than she already had. She stood there, feeling his hand in hers, and she didn't say anything.

"When we kissed on the beach, I felt something there," Scott said gently. "I know you did, too."

Kate couldn't deny what he said. She *had* felt something that day. Standing there with Scott's arms around her and his mouth on hers, she'd felt the way she'd felt the first time he'd kissed her. It had been a dangerous feeling, and that's why she'd pulled away and returned to her friends before anything else could happen.

"That was a mistake, Scott," she said. "It shouldn't have happened."

"But it did happen," Scott replied. "And I think you wanted it to happen. Can you really tell me that you didn't?"

Kate started to speak, then stopped. No, she couldn't really say that she hadn't wanted it to happen. Afterward she'd wished that it hadn't, but right up until the moment their lips had parted she'd been thinking about how nice it felt to be with Scott again. That had been the worst part—not knowing what her true feelings were.

"You don't do things you don't want to, Kate. That's one thing I know about you."

"I didn't say I didn't want to do it at the time," Kate responded. "But that doesn't make it right."

Scott turned her around so that she was facing

him. He dropped the flashlight, the beam of light shooting into the trees beyond them. In the moonlight, the glitter Kate had put on her face sparkled faintly. She saw the outline of Scott's body, felt his hands slide around her waist and pulled her close.

"Maybe you're not sure about it, but I am," he said. "I still feel that way, Kate. I still love you."

He kissed her. Kate shut her eyes as Scott's mouth closed over hers. The warmth of him surrounded her, pressing through the thin fabric of her costume. She felt his fingers on her back and smelled the scent of him. It was a familiar smell, and it brought back a lot of memories.

I still love you. The words broke through the delicious fog that had enveloped Kate's mind like a crack of lightning. Scott had said that he loved her. He'd never said that while they were dating. For a while she'd wanted him to, but he hadn't. Now, right when she most wanted him *not* to say it, he had.

She opened her eyes. Scott had stopped kissing her and was looking at her, smiling. "I knew you felt it," he said.

Kate turned her head away, afraid to keep looking at him. Her eyes followed the flashlight's beam into the trees. Standing there, looking at her, was the raven. Tyler stood among the trees, his eyes fixed on Kate and Scott as they embraced.

Kate pulled away from Scott quickly. "I have to go," she said.

"Please," Scott said. "Don't run away again."

Kate wiped her hand across her mouth. "I have to," she said. "I can't do this."

She looked over again and saw that Tyler had disappeared. Clearly, he had seen her and Scott kissing. Everything was ruined. She had to find him and explain before any more damage was done.

"Kate!" Scott called out as Kate ran into the trees.

She ignored him, running blindly into the darkness in search of Tyler. Her heart ached as she thought about how he must feel after seeing her in Scott's arms. Why had she let Scott kiss her? Why hadn't she fought back?

Because you wanted him to kiss you. The words rang in her head like an accusation. But weren't they at least partially true? Part of her wanted to be back there in Scott's arms. But another part of her was sending her running through the forest in search of someone else.

She heard Scott crashing through the trees behind her, calling out her name. But she didn't stop. She couldn't go back to him. She was afraid of what would happen if she did. And she was afraid of what would happen if she didn't find Tyler and explain things to him soon.

Trees rushed by her as she ran, and several times she stumbled. But somehow she managed to get away from Scott. She saw the beam of his flashlight glinting through the trees behind her, and she was glad that she'd managed to elude him. Now, if only she could find Tyler. She thought about calling to him, but she knew that the sound of her voice would bring Scott running again.

She was completely lost, but it didn't matter. She kept going, turning first one way and then another. Tears ran down her face as she thought about what she'd done and about what it might do to her relationship with Tyler. Why had she been so stupid? Why had she let herself kiss Scott a second time? She was confused, and angry at herself, and all she wanted to do was get away.

After running for ten minutes she stopped, exhausted. She was in a place where the woods opened up a little and allowed more moonlight in. She stood there, getting her bearings and trying not to think about what she'd felt while Scott was kissing her.

You liked it. The same voice that had been taunting her all night came again. *You liked him kissing you.*

She closed her eyes, trying to will the teasing voice away. Yes, she had liked it. Yes, she had felt something. But she didn't want to, and maybe if she tried hard enough she could make herself believe that it hadn't happened.

"Are you lost?"

Kate's eyes flew open. Someone had spoken to her, someone she couldn't see in the darkness of the forest.

"Who's there?" she called softly. "Who said that? Tyler? Is that you?"

A figure stepped from the shadows. Kate backed away hesitantly. Was it Tyler? She couldn't tell. It could even be Scott with his flashlight turned off.

Whoever it was came toward her slowly, in shadows. All she could see at first was a vague outline. But gradually a shape came into view. It was another guy. He was shirtless, and his bare skin shone like pale marble in the moonlight. He had two small horns poking up on either side of his head from a nest of short, curly hair, and a neat goatee covered his chin. Kate couldn't see what kind of pants he had on, but they seemed to be made out of some sort of fuzzy fabric, as if his whole lower body were covered in fur. Something about the costume was familiar. Then Kate realized what it was—he looked like one of the fauns she had seen in pictures illustrating a book of myths she'd had as a little girl. Half human and half goat, the fauns frolicked around in the woods and were always playing tricks on people.

"Are you lost?" the faun asked again, looking at Kate with interest.

"I'm not sure," Kate answered. "Who are you?"

"You look lost," the faun said, not answering her question. "Are you looking for something?"

Kate assumed that the faun was another part of the Midsummer goings-on. She thought his costume was interesting, but she didn't have time for games. She needed to find Tyler.

"I'm looking for someone with a raven mask,"

she said. "Have you seen him?"

The faun shook his head and smiled slyly. "But why would I look for a raven when there's such a beautiful faerie to talk to?" he said.

Kate didn't know what to do next. Scott was somewhere behind her. Tyler was somewhere ahead of her. She didn't know exactly where either one was, and she was stuck in the middle with this guy who couldn't—or wouldn't—tell her anything.

"I should go find my friend," she said, hoping the faun wouldn't be offended if she left him there to play his games with someone else.

"Won't you stay and talk to me for a while?" he asked, sounding disappointed.

"I don't really have time," Kate answered.

The faun looked at her sadly. "Maybe I can help you find what you're looking for," he said eagerly.

"I doubt it," Kate said. "Not unless you've seen the guy with the raven mask."

"Sometimes masks hide the truth," replied the faun. "I asked you *what* you're looking for, not *who*."

Great, Kate thought. *Another one who likes to talk nonsense.* She didn't need riddles. She needed answers. Better yet, she needed directions. She had no idea where she was, no idea where Tyler was, and no idea how to get where she wanted to be.

"Kate?" Scott's voice echoed through the woods. It sounded as if he was right behind her. She looked around frantically. If he found her he would just start trying to get her to come back to him all over again. She needed to get away. But where would she go?

"Come," the faun said. "I can help you."

Kate glanced at him. She didn't know anything about him. What if he got her even more lost?

"Kate?" Scott was getting closer. She could see the beam from his flashlight moving toward her.

"Come," the faun said again, holding out his hand.

Kate reached out to take it, but at the last minute she pulled away. Something about the faun was appealing, but she still didn't know if he could be trusted. "Thanks," she said. "I think I can manage."

She turned and ran into the darkness, leaving the faun and Scott behind her.

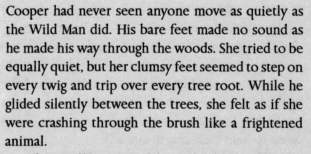

CHAPTER 9

Cooper had never seen anyone move as quietly as the Wild Man did. His bare feet made no sound as he made his way through the woods. She tried to be equally quiet, but her clumsy feet seemed to step on every twig and trip over every tree root. While he glided silently between the trees, she felt as if she were crashing through the brush like a frightened animal.

This really irritated her. She knew that the others wanted her to fail whatever stupid test they'd set up for her, and she wanted to show them up. To make things worse, her supposed guide gave her no indication of where they were going. He just walked. Spider had said that a guide would lead her into the realm of Faerie. What had he meant by that? They were still in the same old woods they'd been in all evening. Was there something waiting for her there—another surprise, perhaps? Where were all the others? Would the Wild Man tell her?

Was he bringing her to them? Could he even speak? He hadn't made so much as a grunt yet.

The Wild Man stopped walking. He turned to Cooper and pointed to something beside him. Cooper looked and realized that they were standing beside a stream. The water in it was running low, and the banks were exposed, revealing thick mud. The Wild Man pointed again. What did he mean? Was she supposed to do something with the mud?

The Wild Man pointed to his skin and pantomimed rubbing mud on his body. Now Cooper understood. He wanted her to do the same thing. But she didn't want to. She was comfortable just the way she was. She didn't want to be filthy. Why did she have to make herself up like the Wild Man? She suspected that he and his buddies were just trying to make her look even more foolish, and she didn't want to help them out in any way.

The Wild Man sensed her hesitation and pointed again to the mud. Cooper shook her head, and this time the Wild Man splashed into the water, picked up a handful of mud, and smeared it over his face and chest. The mud was a reddish brown color, and it contrasted with the dried gray mud that already stained his skin.

Cooper watched as he rubbed mud in his hair and over the rest of himself until he was covered from head to toe in it. He motioned for her to join him in the stream. She started to protest, but then she stopped herself. She had told Bird and Spider that she could do this. She'd promised to see the challenges through. What would they think if she backed out at the very first one? Maybe there really was some point to getting muddy.

With a sigh, she removed her shoes and stepped into the water. It was cooler than she would have expected for summertime. The Wild Man picked up a handful of mud and handed it to her. She took it from him, feeling the coldness of it on her skin and smelling the rich, earthy scent that rose from it. As he watched, she smeared it on her arm in thick strokes. He nodded approvingly, and she dug her fingers into the mud to get another handful. This she wiped on her legs, covering them in the red color.

To her surprise, she quickly got into playing in the mud. There was something childlike about it, something primitive and pure that made her feel both happy and secure. She scooped up more and more of it, rubbing it across her chest and over the dress of her costume until she was almost entirely covered in it. Then she picked up more and worked it into her hair, twisting it into spikes and cork-screws that stuck out wildly from her head.

Her face was last, and she carefully smoothed a film of the mud over her features, being sure not to get it in her eyes or mouth. Throughout the process the Wild Man stood watching her silently. When she was done, he stepped out of the stream and motioned for her to do the same. She left her shoes behind as he led her a little farther downstream to where the water fanned out into a shallow pool. He knelt and motioned for her to do the same. Then he pointed at the surface of the pool.

Cooper looked at her own reflection. Her muddied face stared back at her, the eyes large blinking circles surrounded by the reddish dirt that had already dried in the warm air. Her hair was a mess, twisted and matted with thick gobs of clay. The Wild Man's reflection was beside hers, and she couldn't help but notice how similar they looked now that she had become a creature of the earth, too.

A creature of the earth. The phrase stuck in her mind. That really was what she'd become—a thing made out of dirt. She turned to the Wild Man. "Is that what this is about" she asked him, "understanding the element of earth?" Wicca was about the cycles of nature, after all. Maybe her test was to experience the elements one at a time or something.

The Wild Man didn't respond. Instead, he took something out of a pouch that hung at his side and handed it to Cooper. It was a piece of charred stick.

"What am I supposed to do with this?" she asked.

The Wild Man pretended to draw on his skin with his finger. Now Cooper understood. He wanted her to draw on the dried clay that covered her skin. But why? What was she supposed to draw?

She thought for a moment. Then, using the pool as a mirror, she drew a spiral shape on her forehead. "It represents the universe," she said. It also reminded her of the spiral dances they sometimes did in rituals. Then she drew some star shapes around the spiral. After that she found herself drawing random designs all over herself. She drew lines on her arms and squiggles on her legs. She drew circles and triangles and more stars. She just let her mind run free, and soon she was decorated with all kinds of strange things.

"How's that?" she asked the Wild Man when she was done. She wanted to know if she was doing things the right way. But he gave her no indication of being either pleased or dissatisfied with what she'd done. He just looked at her with his deep, dark eyes and then took the piece of charred stick from her and returned it to his bag.

He began to walk again. Once more Cooper followed. The mud cracked a little as she walked, forming networks of tiny lines across her skin. She liked how it felt. It was as if she'd been made out of the earth itself, formed from the same stuff that made the mountains and rocks. She thought about pictures she'd seen of primitive people, their bodies painted in much the same way hers now was. They'd always looked so strange to her, like things that had crept out of the ground or perhaps the spirits of the land. Yes, that's how she felt—like some kind of wood spirit. She'd thought her

nymph costume had been about becoming a creature of the forest, but this was even better. Now her
costume, all covered in mud, was unrecognizable,
but she felt more disguised in just the mud than she
had in the makeup and material.

The longer she walked through the forest with
the Wild Man, the more she felt like a wild animal
herself. Her bare feet felt every stone and pine nee-
dle. She smelled like the mud, and she blended into
the woods in a way that she hadn't before. She
began to notice that many of the forest animals
around them didn't run when they passed by. Was it
because they sensed she was more like them now?
By covering up her normal smell with the smell of
the earth, had she become that much more like
something untamed? The idea of it excited her.

The Wild Man was walking more slowly now.
He was also sniffing the air, his nose twitching as
the breeze blew by them. Cooper sniffed, too, but
all she smelled was mud. What was the Wild Man
looking for?

The Wild Man looked at Cooper and then
crouched on the ground, where he began to draw
something in the dirt with a stick. She knelt beside
him, looking at the picture he was making. It looked
like some kind of circle with four sticks coming out
of the bottom. Then he added another circle to it,
and suddenly Cooper knew what it was. Or at least
she thought she did.

"Is it a pig?" she said.

The Wild Man nodded. But Cooper was confused. He was sniffing the air for the scent of a pig? They didn't have pigs in the woods. At least not the tame kind.

"A wild pig?" she tried again. "A boar?"

The Wild Man nodded enthusiastically.

"There's a boar in the forest?" Cooper asked. That didn't seem possible. There were no boars in the woods they were in. She didn't know if there were any boars living in *any* forests, for that matter. At least not anymore. She remembered reading about people going boar hunting in a book she had about Camelot and the knights of the Round Table, but that was in England. And it was hundreds of years ago. And it was fiction.

The Wild Man drew some more pictures. These were smaller circles with what looked like floppy ears. They were running after the boar.

"Dogs," Cooper said. "There are dogs hunting the boar. Is that right?"

Again, the Wild Man nodded in the affirmative, and again he drew a picture. This was unmistakably a horse, and there was someone sitting on it. But who was it? Cooper was already puzzled over the fact that her meditation had taken such a strange turn. She tried to think of what she knew about boars and hunting and Midsummer.

Something came to her suddenly, something Annie had been telling them on the drive up. She'd been reading up on Midsummer legends, and she'd said something about hunting. What had it been? Cooper had been caught up in the CD that had been playing and hadn't heard all of what Annie was saying. But she remembered it because one of the phrases had struck her as sounding really cool.

The Wild Hunt. That was it. Annie had mentioned something about the Wild Hunt. But what had she said exactly? Cooper thought hard. Herne. That was the other name. Herne and the Wild Hunt. It all came back to her now. There was a legend that on Midsummer Eve the immortal hunter Herne took his pack of dogs through the woods in search of a magical boar. She couldn't remember why, but that wasn't the important part.

"Is it the Wild Hunt?" she asked the Wild Man.

He answered her by tossing the stick away and standing up. Cooper stood, too. The Wild Man was very still, his head tilted to one side. Cooper listened, and soon she heard the sounds of something running through the woods toward them. Then she heard the unmistakable sound of dogs baying. At least it sort of sounded like dogs. It was more like people pretending to be dogs. The more she listened, the more the noises sounded like people running through the woods and barking.

"What's going on?" Cooper asked the Wild Man. "Who's making all that noise?"

The Wild Man pointed once more to the pictures he'd drawn in the dirt.

"The Wild Hunt?" Cooper said. "But those don't sound like real dogs."

Then, suddenly, she got it. "It's people acting out the Wild Hunt, isn't it?" she said.

The Wild Man nodded.

"It's Spider and the others," Cooper continued, piecing together the bits of information she had and filling in the empty spaces with her own ideas. "This is all part of the ritual, right? We're acting out the Wild Hunt?"

Again the Wild Man nodded.

"What do we do?" Cooper asked.

Something crashed through the brush off to their right, making Cooper jump. Was it one of the kids pretending to be a dog? She didn't see anything. But the gathering dusk made it more difficult to tell what was going on. It could have been someone running, but it could have been something else as well.

The Wild Man began walking quickly, motioning for Cooper to do the same. Together they crept through the woods. Cooper could hear the sounds of the "dogs" getting closer. Then she heard a man's voice call out, "Boar ahead, dogs. On the scent!"

That must be Herne, she thought excitedly. The voice sounded a lot like Spider's. That would make sense. As the leader of the group, he would naturally want to be the star of the ritual. Part of her wanted to stop and wait for him to arrive. But another part was frightened at the sound of his voice. That part of her urged her to run away. That seemed like an odd response to her. Why would she want to run from Spider? But she did.

The sound of the hounds—which was how Cooper thought of the people pretending to be dogs—was coming closer and closer. She heard them running now, their feet crashing through the brush. She heard, too, Spider urging them on.

"Up ahead!" he shouted. "The boar, dogs. The boar is close by."

What was all of this about a boar? Cooper didn't understand, any more than she understood why the Wild Man was running away from Spider and the others and why she was following him. Shouldn't they wait to join them? After all, wasn't the point of her becoming a wild thing like the others so that she could join them in the hunt and become part of the group? She had covered herself in mud, and now she was ready for the rest of the test. If it meant pretending to be a hound and chasing after some made-up magical boar, she was all set.

She herself felt like an animal. The mud on her body was beginning to itch a little, and the smell was growing stronger. But the pain in her bare feet reminded her that she was still a soft human and not totally a creature of the forest. Unlike them, she couldn't run on all fours without feeling it in every step. She wished she hadn't left her shoes behind, and she wanted to go back for them. She looked ahead to see where the Wild Man was, but he had disappeared in the falling night. She could see a vague shadow ahead of her, but that was all.

A moment later she heard the "dogs" running through the woods behind her and Spider calling, "There she is, hounds. The Midsummer boar is ours."

The "dogs" let out yips of excitement, and Cooper heard the woods around her rustle as they crashed through the trees. What did Spider mean by saying the boar was theirs? There was no boar. Besides, she hadn't even joined the game yet. It couldn't possibly be over before she'd even had a chance to play.

Then a horrible thought came to her. *I'm the Midsummer boar*, she thought, suddenly understanding what was going on. Spider was pretending to be the hunter Herne. The others were pretending to be hounds hunting the Midsummer boar. And she was what they were hunting. She didn't know why, and she didn't know what it meant, but she knew it was the truth. She was being hunted by the pack of kids Bird had introduced her to. They weren't waiting for her to join them, they were trying to catch her.

To make things worse, she was alone. The Wild Man had deserted her. Her next thought was that *this*, finally, was the test she'd been brought to this place to take. She really had become a creature of the forest, even if it was all pretend. For what purpose, she didn't know. All she knew was that now she was being hunted by a pack of "dogs" that was almost upon her. Realizing it, she did what any wild pig would do—she turned and ran.

CHAPTER 10

Annie stood and followed Robin Hood. She couldn't help but wonder how she'd become involved in the ritual in the first place. Had someone really selected her? If so, who? Was it someone from the Coven of the Green Wood, or someone from Crones' Circle? Why would they pick her? These questions filled her head as she and Robin walked across the clearing and into the woods, following the departing Oak King.

In the woods, Annie saw that there was another tent set up. Like the one she'd found the king in, this one was made out of yellow and orange material. As they went inside, Annie reflected on the fact that whoever had staged the ceremony had gone through a lot of trouble.

Inside the tent, she found several other people. They sat the Oak King in a chair and began to do various things to him. Some washed his hands and face with water from a bowl. Others combed his hair and beard and tied them with yellow and red ribbons.

"What are we supposed to do?" Annie whispered to Robin.

"Wait until he commands us," Robin said softly.

The attendants fussed over the king for a while, grooming him and bringing him new robes to put on. These were made of beautiful yellow satin embroidered all over with red and orange swirls that reminded Annie of suns. When he turned and stood before Annie and Robin he seemed to glow. He looked younger and stronger than he had all evening. Gazing at him, Annie couldn't believe that anyone thought he would lose in a battle.

"My brother will be here shortly," the king said. "I will not have time to speak with you again once things begin. I want to thank you both for your service to me—Robin during my reign, and you, little hedgehog, on this most important of nights."

"It was my pleasure, my lord," said Robin. "I look forward to serving you again upon your return."

The Oak King turned to Annie. "I hope to see you again as well someday," he said. "You have been most brave."

"I haven't done anything," Annie said.

"But you have," said the Oak King. "You allowed yourself to face a great fear. That is a very brave thing indeed."

Annie knew that he was talking about the

deaths of her parents. But she hadn't faced that, and she certainly didn't feel brave. Still, she didn't want to contradict the king.

"Soon I will face my brother," the king continued. "And I will die."

"No," Annie said suddenly. "Don't say that." She was surprised at her outburst, but as she stood looking at the faces of the king and Robin, both of whom were watching her with interest, she realized that she didn't want the Oak King to die, even if it was just a game. He was so handsome and so kind. She didn't want to think of him dead. It would remind her too much of her father and that sometimes she wanted more than anything for him to hold her again and tell her that everything was okay.

She was afraid she was going to start crying. She felt like a little kid, getting so upset about the death of someone she didn't even know, especially when she knew he wasn't really going to die. But she was upset nonetheless.

"Robin, leave us for a moment," the Oak King said.

Robin bowed and exited the tent, taking with him the king's attendants so that only the Oak King and Annie remained. When everyone was gone, the king walked over to Annie.

"You were selected for this task for a reason," he said. "You have shown that you are more than prepared to do what needs to be done. I knew that when I offered you a chance to leave me and you chose to stay. But now the hardest part is almost here. Be brave, little hedgehog. There is much for you to learn if you are willing."

Annie didn't respond. There didn't seem to be anything to say. The king was right—she'd come this far, now she would have to see the ritual through to the end, no matter how many bad memories it brought up or how much she didn't want to do it. She would just have to keep telling herself that it wasn't real.

"I can do it," she said, as much to herself as to the king.

The tent flaps opened, and Robin poked his head in. "My lord," he said. "The Holly King has arrived."

The king looked at Annie. "You have been my squire all night," he said. "I hope that you will be by my side now. Will you?"

Annie looked into his face. His eyes were shining. She thought about how he had held her when she'd been crying. It reminded her of the way her father had held her that night long ago when her life had changed—when everything had changed.

"Yes," she said. "I will."

The king smiled and gave her a hug. His arms circled her, and she felt him pull her close. For a moment she felt as if she were in her father's arms again. Then he released her.

"Walk ahead of me, little hedgehog," the king said. "Perform this final duty with honor."

Annie left the tent and walked back to the gathering place. When she entered the clearing ahead of the Oak King, she was amazed at how it had been transformed during the time they had been in the King's tent. Gone was the table, and there were no signs that a party had taken place there only half an hour before. More torches had been added, and they burned with a magical brightness that made it seem almost like midday.

At the far end of the clearing, green-and-white banners fluttered from poles that had been stuck into the ground. Standing beneath them was a large man dressed in the same colors. Annie knew instantly that he was the Holly King. He looked a great deal like his brother, but his hair and beard were a deep auburn color instead of the gray of the Oak King's. Standing beside him was a young girl in a green robe. She was wearing a wreath of holly leaves on her head, and four tiny candles burned at equal intervals around it.

"I see you made it," the Holly King called out in a loud, jolly voice. Annie was surprised at how nice he sounded. For some reason she'd expected him to be mean.

"Indeed," the Oak King bellowed back. "Have I ever missed one of our meetings?"

Both brothers laughed, filling the clearing with the sound of their voices. *Maybe this won't be so bad after all*, Annie thought. They seemed to be in high spirits, and she hoped that she would be able to get herself into the mood of the game once it began.

Banners with the Oak King's colors had been erected across from those of the Holly King. Robin stood beneath them, awaiting the king and Annie. When they walked over to him, he held out a large, gleaming sword.

"Your weapon, my lord," he said to the king.

The Oak King took the sword and held it in his hands, testing the weight. A smile darted across his face as he swung it several times.

"You've kept it well," he said to Robin. "I don't suppose you've been practicing with it a bit?"

"Perhaps a bit," Robin said mischievously.

"You will keep it safe for me until my return, I trust," said the king.

"Perhaps your squire should keep it for you instead," Robin replied, nodding at Annie.

The Oak King smiled. "My squire has more important duties than polishing swords," he answered. "She will have much work to do while I am away."

"Work?" Annie said. "What kind of work?"

"You'll have to wait and find out," the king said. "But now I need you to hold my crown." He bent down so that Annie could remove the garland of oak leaves and acorns from his head. When she had taken it, the Oak King looked deep into her eyes and said, "Don't fear for me."

He stood and turned to face his brother, who was standing across the clearing with his own sword in his hands. "Are you ready, Brother?" he called.

"If you are ready, I am ready," the Holly King answered.

The two men strode into the center of the clearing and stopped. The crowd of people formed a circle around them, closing them in. There was total silence as everyone waited to see what was going to happen next.

"It has been six months since you took from me the crown of winter and replaced it with the crown of spring," the Holly King said. "Will you now accept my challenge as I avenge my defeat and reclaim what is mine?"

The Oak King stood tall and proud as he said, "I accept your challenge, Brother, as I have each time before this."

The two brothers embraced one another, then stepped apart. At an invisible signal, each raised his sword and began to circle. They moved around one another in a slow dance, only their legs moving as they circled in the center of the ring. Annie watched them closely, wondering how often they'd had to practice the routine to get it right. The swords might not be real swords, but they certainly looked heavy and sharp. One wrong whack with one of them and someone could easily get hurt.

The Oak King was the first to strike, swinging his sword at his brother's neck. Annie closed her eyes, afraid that the Holly King's head was going to go flying. Then she remembered that it was all an act and she relaxed. Besides, the Holly King had deflected the swipe with his own sword and his brother's sword had simply glanced off.

Once more the two kings circled one another, each waiting for an opportunity to attack the other. Their expressions were intense as they stared into one another's eyes. Annie could feel the electricity in the summer air as she watched, the Oak King's crown clutched in her fingers. Silently, she urged him on, wanting him to win. Even though everyone said that he had to lose, she didn't believe it. She knew that he could do it.

Her wish seemed to be coming true when the Oak King leapt forward and landed a blow on his brother's arm. Annie let out a little yelp as she saw it happen, unable to contain her excitement. But the next minute the Holly King had struck the Oak King in the side, and her king was backing away. Was he in pain? Was he hurt? Annie wanted to run out to help him.

He faltered but regained his stance, charging at the Holly King with his sword pointed at his chest. The Holly King charged in turn, and the two clashed together in the center of the clearing like two trains colliding. The air filled with the sound of metal on metal as their swords hit. Annie held her breath, wondering if either had been hurt. But when they separated she saw that they were both fine.

Then they began fighting in earnest, swinging at one another just like actors in a scene from a movie. The Holly King's sword slashed across his brother's robe, cutting it. *Maybe those swords are sharper than they look*, Annie thought as the Oak King brought his weapon up and neatly hooked his opponent's forearm. But when no blood appeared Annie felt reassured that the swords were just props.

As the battle raged, she looked around at the faces of the people in the clearing. They all seemed very somber, not at all like the laughing, happy people who had been telling jokes and singing earlier in the evening. It was almost as if they were watching something very serious, and not a performance created for a Midsummer celebration. Even Robin, standing by her side and watching the kings fight, seemed to be lost in some kind of trance.

There was a sharp gasp from the crowd, and Annie looked up to see what had happened. The Oak King was on one knee, holding himself up with his sword. The Holly King was standing in front of him, his sword raised in the air. What had happened? Had the Oak King been struck? Annie couldn't tell. She cursed herself for having turned her eyes away.

The Oak King looked up into his brother's face. "And so it ends," he said in a clear, strong voice.

"Yes," the Holly King said. "Good-bye, Brother. Until we meet again."

Annie knew then that the Oak King was going to lose, just as everyone had said he would. She knew that, for whatever reason, this was how the fight was supposed to end, but she still wasn't able to accept it.

"No!" she cried, breaking the stillness in the clearing. "No. You have to fight. You have to win. I know you can do it. Get up."

She began to run onto the field, to run to the Oak King and urge him to stand up again. But Robin grabbed her and held her back, his strong hands closing on her shoulders as she tried to break free.

"No," she said again. Everyone was staring at her, but she didn't care. She didn't want the Oak King to lose.

The Holly King looked over at her, his dark eyes meeting hers. For a moment she thought that he was going to put down his sword and end the battle. He seemed to understand her pain, and she couldn't believe that he would do anything to hurt the Oak King, even in a pretend fight.

But then he looked away and brought his sword down. Annie closed her eyes and screamed, not able to watch. When she opened them again a few moments later, the Oak King was stretched out on the ground. The Holly King's attendant had run to his side, and he was leaning down so that she could place a crown of shiny green holly leaves and bright red berries on his head.

Annie broke free from Robin's grasp and ran to the fallen Oak King. She knelt by his side. There was no blood anywhere, no sign that anything had really happened except for a tear in the king's robe. It really *had* all been a performance. She didn't know why she'd let herself get so carried away. She felt stupid. But it had all felt so real for a moment.

She looked at the king's face, with its peaceful smile and closed eyes. She knew he would open them when he felt her beside him. Then she could tell him how amazing it had been, how well he and the man playing the Holly King had performed their roles. She knelt there, looking down and waiting for him to come back to her.

"He's gone, child," the Holly King said, kneeling beside her. "He's gone to await his time."

"It's okay," Annie said to him. "You don't have to keep pretending. You guys did a great job. I wish Kate and Cooper could have seen it."

Robin joined them in kneeling beside the Oak King. "You did well," he told Annie. "Now it is time for us to send him on his way."

He helped her to stand up. But she still didn't understand. Clearly, the Oak King wasn't really dead. They wouldn't let that happen. But he wasn't moving. It was like he was asleep. What was going on? Why wasn't he getting up? Robin pulled her to one side, where they stood with Maid Marian as the Holly King stood over his brother.

"The old magic has been fulfilled," he cried out. "The Oak King is dead. Now is the time of the Holly King."

The people around them cheered. Annie didn't understand. Why were they cheering for the person who had killed their king? It didn't make sense. They had eaten at the Oak King's table. They'd sung songs about him. They'd laughed at the skit that made fun of the Holly King. But here they were, calling out the Holly King's name. Even Marian and Robin were laughing and cheering.

"How can you?" she asked angrily. "How can you cheer for him?" She knew it was all make-believe, but it still upset her.

"Quiet," Marian told her. "There is more."

As Annie looked on, six figures walked into the clearing. She couldn't tell if they were women or men because they were wearing masks. Each mask was different, but each was an animal from the forest. There was a stag, a bear, a fox, a hare, a bird, and, coming at the end of the procession, a hedgehog.

"That's my mask!" Annie said. She had left it at the table when she'd gone to help the Oak King prepare for the battle. Someone must have picked it up and decided to wear it.

The six animals were carrying a long, flat object that looked like several thin saplings lashed together with rope to form a crude sort of stretcher. They walked over to the Oak King and laid the thing on the ground. Then they lifted him onto it and arranged his hands over his chest. Throughout the whole thing the man playing the Oak King never moved. He really did seem to be dead, which made Annie feel sadder than she knew she probably should.

The animal-faced people lifted the Oak King, each one holding the stretcher at a different point, like pallbearers at a funeral. As they carried him out of the clearing they sang.

> Gone away, beloved king.
> Sleep and dream while winter storms.
> With the Goddess you are resting,
> cradled in her loving arms.

The song was sung like a lullaby, the six voices gentle and soothing. Annie could almost picture the Oak King being held by the Goddess as a mother would hold a baby she was comforting. It made her feel better, and it also made her feel a little sad. Many times she'd fallen asleep in her own mother's arms after having a nightmare or a stomachache. She missed that.

The animal people disappeared into the woods with the Oak King, but Annie could still hear them singing as they walked away from the clearing. Where were they taking the Oak King? What would they do with him? Would he reappear later at the big Midsummer dance? She hoped so. She wanted to have the chance to tell him how much she'd enjoyed the ritual and what it had shown her about herself.

She still didn't really understand the ritual. Why were people celebrating the fact that the king was dead? That didn't fit anything she'd ever heard about Wicca or experienced in any of the rituals she'd been involved in. Witchcraft was all about celebrating life. Death wasn't something that was supposed to make people happy. She certainly didn't feel happy watching everyone make a big fuss over the Holly King.

She walked away from the crowd and sat beneath the banners of the Oak King. They hung limply, barely moving in the breeze. As Annie sat, watching everyone crowd around the new king of the woods, she found herself wanting to run after the six people who had carried the king away. It reminded her too much of having her parents taken away from her before she really had a chance to say everything that she wanted to say. No one was mourning the king's death. They were too busy having another party to even think about him, or at least that's what it seemed like to her.

"Why are you not joining in the festivities?" someone asked her.

She looked up. Standing over her was the Holly King. His fighting robes had been replaced by much finer ones of dark green and silver. In his hand was a cup, and he seemed in fine spirits.

"I don't really feel like it," Annie said.

The Holly King nodded. "The death of my brother has upset you," he said.

"I know it's all just a game," said Annie. "But I don't understand. Why doesn't anyone seem to care? Why did the Oak King have to die? Why do you get to win?"

"For the same reason that my brother will win at Yule and I will die," the Holly King answered. "That is the way of it. A king must die in order that his people may live."

Annie sighed. She still didn't get it. "I still don't like it," she said.

The Holly King held out his hand. "Come with me," he said. "There is something I want to show you."

Annie wasn't at all sure that she wanted to go with the Holly King. Actor or not, he had just pretended to kill someone she really liked. She knew that being angry at him was like being angry at the villains on a soap opera, but she couldn't help seeing him as a traitor.

"Please," the Holly King said, sensing her hesitation. "I think this will help you understand."

Reluctantly, Annie reached out and took the king's hand, and he helped her to her feet. The Holly King took one of the torches, and he and Annie walked together out of the clearing, leaving the noise of the party behind them. As they passed beneath the trees at the edge of the circle, Annie thought how odd it was that she had entered the clearing with the Oak King and now she was leaving it with the Holly King, his brother—and his murderer.

CHAPTER II

It was getting late. The moon was high overhead, and Kate was tired. She was also lost. She'd wandered in the woods for what seemed like hours without seeing anyone. She knew she should have run into other Midsummer revelers, or even into some random campers, but she'd seen no one. It was as if she was somehow being led deeper and deeper into the woods and farther and farther away from where she wanted to be. She'd left Scott and his flashlight behind long ago, and she hadn't caught even a glimpse of Tyler.

She had been walking gradually uphill for some time, and now she found herself at the top of a small rise. The other side sloped steeply down, and she couldn't see what waited for her at the bottom. She didn't think she wanted to find out. All she wanted to do was get back to familiar faces and have a drink. Her throat was parched, and she was exhausted from all the walking.

She sat down on a fallen log to rest and get her

bearings. Her feet hurt, and she knew her hair and makeup probably looked terrible. If she didn't find her way back soon she was going to miss the big dance, too, and then her whole trip would be ruined. *As if it isn't already ruined*, she told herself miserably. She was alone, Tyler was gone, and Scott had made her think about things she didn't want to think about.

"Stupid boys," she said as she stood up. She was angry again, and determined to find her way out of the forest. She didn't care if she found Tyler or not, and she wasn't about to have her dance ruined because of him or Scott.

As she stood up her foot slipped, and she found herself sliding backward. She was going down the hill. She tried to grab on to something to stop her fall, but her hand closed on empty air. Then she began to roll, her body tumbling over the pine needles. In the dark she couldn't tell which way was up and which was down, and before she knew it she was lying at the bottom of the hill in a heap.

After a moment she sat up. Luckily, the pine needles were fairly soft, and she hadn't been hurt. She was just roughed up a little, all except her wings, which were bent. For some reason that was the last straw. Kate found herself crying, and she couldn't stop. She sat in the needles, her broken wings hanging limply at her sides, and the tears rolled down her cheeks. A moment later someone was kneeling beside her and brushing her face with a gentle hand.

"Are you all right?" a concerned voice asked.

Kate looked up into the face of the faun. His nose was only inches away, and his dark eyes stared down at her. For a moment she was almost frightened, but he sounded so worried that instead she just felt grateful to see a familiar face.

"I'm okay," she said. "It's really just my costume that got damaged."

"I came looking for you after you ran off," the faun said. "I was worried that you might get hurt."

Kate sniffled. "Thanks," she said. "But I'm all right." She was glad that the organizers of the evening were at least watching out for the people in the woods.

The faun crouched down on the ground next to her, peering at her through the gloom. "I don't think you're all right," he said.

"No, really," Kate said. "I'm fine. Thanks for helping me though."

She tried to stand and winced as pain shot through her leg. She sat down again with a huff. "Or maybe I'm not fine," she said. "I think I bruised something. It should be okay if I just sit for a while."

The two of them sat in silence for a minute. Kate was glad that the faun was there, but she was also a little uneasy about sitting in the dark with him. Why had he followed her? Had he really been concerned for her welfare, or did he have other motives? Something about him unnerved her a little bit. But was it him, or was it something about herself that was troubling her?

"Can I ask why you were running away?" the faun said suddenly.

Kate sighed. She really didn't want to talk about the subject, especially with a stranger. At the same time, though, she knew that there really wasn't anyone else she could talk about it with. Cooper and Annie were her best friends, but she wasn't sure this was something she wanted to discuss with them. She couldn't talk to her mother, as much as she loved talking to her. And she certainly couldn't talk to the two guys at the center of her emotional storm. Maybe spilling her soul to a stranger in the middle of the woods was exactly what she did need.

"I was trying to find someone I really love and trying to get away from someone else who wants me to love him," she said.

"And you don't love this other person?" asked the faun.

Kate didn't know how to answer that question. Did she love Scott? She had once, and she certainly liked kissing him. But did she love him?

"I don't think so," she said.

"But you aren't sure?" the faun pressed, thoughtfully scratching his beard.

"Maybe I don't really know what being in love is," answered Kate. "I thought it meant wanting to be with someone so much that no one else could get your attention. Now I'm not sure."

"This person you think you love," said the faun, "why do you think that?"

Kate thought about Tyler. She pictured his face as he told her a joke, and imagined holding hands with him as they stood in a ritual circle. She thought about how happy it made her when he called, and how she liked discussing Wicca with him.

"He makes me feel good about myself," Kate said, more to herself than to the faun. "He makes me think that I can do anything I want to."

"And the other person?" the faun continued.

Now, Kate thought about Scott. She thought about how it felt to be held by him, and how time seemed to stop when he kissed her. She remembered how excited she'd been when he'd finally asked her out; she'd felt like the most beautiful girl in school.

"He makes me feel special," said Kate. "He makes me feel pretty."

The faun didn't say anything. Kate looked over at him and saw that his head was hanging down as if he was sad. Had she said something wrong?

"Now you're the one who doesn't look fine," she said teasingly.

The faun looked up. "I was just thinking that the

one you love is very lucky," he said.

Kate looked away. She felt self-conscious. Here she was, telling a total stranger her most intimate thoughts. It was a good thing she didn't really know him. If she did, she would find it hard to face him at the end of the evening.

"Have you ever been in love?" she asked him, curious to hear his answer.

"Yes," the faun said. "With a beautiful girl."

"What happened?" Kate asked when the faun didn't continue.

"She ran away," he said simply.

Kate wanted to say something comforting, but she didn't know what to say. Was the faun telling her the truth, or was he just making up a story to go along with his character? She didn't know the answer to that.

"I'm sorry," she said, not knowing what else to say. Then she stretched her leg and found that it didn't hurt quite as much as it had before. "I think I can walk now," she said. "Shall we try to head back?"

The faun got up and offered her his hand. She took it and got to her feet. There was a little bit of pain when she put her weight on her foot, but she would be fine. She looked up the steep hill and sighed. "Here goes nothing," she said.

She and the faun climbed slowly up the hill, with Kate leaning on his shoulder whenever the climb got too difficult. She couldn't believe he was doing all of that climbing so easily, but he didn't seem to be having any trouble. When they finally reached the top, she paused to catch her breath.

"Remind me not to go on any more nature hikes by myself in the dark," she said jokingly.

They began to walk back through the woods. Kate didn't know if they were going in the right direction, but she assumed the faun knew where they were headed. They walked slowly because her leg was still a little sore, and from time to time she needed to take the faun's hand when they went down an incline.

"I don't know who you are," Kate said to him at one point, "but you're the nicest faun I've ever met. Thanks again for helping me."

"It's my pleasure," he answered. "Perhaps in return you would give me a little gift?"

Kate was puzzled. "But I don't have anything," she said.

The faun smiled. "You have a kiss," he said.

Kate felt herself blushing. The faun was looking at her, his dark eyes twinkling.

"I told you that I once loved a beautiful girl who ran away," the faun said. "That girl is you."

Kate laughed. "That's a line if I ever heard one," she said. "How can you love someone you just met?"

"But I do," the faun said. "I know your heart

belongs to another, but perhaps you will give me just one small kiss?"

Kate looked at him. He *was* really cute. For a faun. Would it hurt to give him just one kiss? At first she thought it wouldn't. Then she remembered how one small kiss with Scott had turned into a great big problem.

"I'm sorry," she said. "I don't think it's a good idea."

The faun sighed. "You've broken my heart," he said sadly, but Kate had the feeling he was being overly dramatic as part of the game.

The faun continued walking. "We're almost there now," he said cheerfully, seeming to have forgotten already all about how she'd broken his heart.

Kate breathed a sigh of relief. Finally, her nightmare was almost over. All she wanted to do was get back to the cabin, clean up, maybe get something to eat and drink, and then join her friends for the big dance. *Who knows what kind of excitement I missed while I was out in those woods*, she thought bitterly. Cooper and Annie had probably been off having all kinds of fun without her. Even Tyler was probably having fun without her. And what was she doing? Spending her evening with a faun. *Just what a faerie princess would wish for*, she thought.

They had reached a part of the woods that Kate thought she recognized. At least now they were on a trail instead of just walking blindly through the trees. She could probably make it on her own from there.

She was about to tell the faun that she could go the rest of the way by herself when suddenly she saw lights twinkling in the darkness. They were floating in the air, flickering softly and hovering at various heights. It took Kate a moment to realize that they were fireflies.

"Look at that," she said to the faun. "I've never seen so many in one place."

But instead of being excited about the intriguing sight, the faun seemed startled. He stopped, pulling away from Kate.

"I have to leave you now," he said. "But you'll be fine. Just keep following the path."

Before Kate could stop him, he turned and dashed back into the darkness. *Why does everyone run away from me?* she asked herself. First Tyler and now the faun. She was starting to take it personally. The only person who seemed to want to be around her was Scott, and he was the one person she didn't want to see.

The fireflies grew nearer, and as they did Kate saw that they were all forming a tighter and tighter group. In fact, they seemed to be taking shape. They were still too far away for her to really tell what was happening, but it certainly looked like the light was becoming something more solid.

Then, as suddenly as they had appeared, the lights went out. The plunge into blackness was disorienting, and Kate stood in one spot, blinking as her eyes adjusted to the darkness once more. When she could see again, she was surprised to find that the two children she had seen emerge from beneath Maeve's skirts were standing in front of her.

"Hi," she said. "How'd you do that trick with the lights? And isn't it a little late for the two of you to be out here?"

The girl and the boy looked at one another and laughed. Then they turned back to Kate.

"Maeve requests your presence," they said in unison. "Come with us."

Without waiting for an answer, they turned and walked away hand in hand. Kate looked at their retreating backs, trying to decide what to do. She really wanted to get back to the cabin. She was tired of these games, even if the people involved were really good at it. Would they be upset if she skipped this part of things? Surely no one would notice. Besides, her wings were broken. She didn't want people to see her looking like that.

Then again, it might be interesting. So far Maeve had been the most spectacular part of the celebration. Kate wouldn't mind seeing what tricks she had up her sleeve. And it probably wouldn't take all that long. She could go see what was happening, race back to the cabin, and get back in time for the dance. When would she ever have another chance to see something like this?

She made up her mind. Trying not to run too much because of her leg, she hobbled after the two kids. "Hey!" she called out. "Wait for me."

CHAPTER 12

As she darted through the forest, racing around trees and ducking under low-lying limbs, Cooper stole quick glances over her shoulder. Each time, the "dogs" seemed to get closer and closer. They had seen her, and it had thrown them into a frenzy. They leaped and crashed through the forest, bounding over logs and running around anything that was too heavy to knock over or too tall to jump. They yipped and barked in their human voices, but she still thought of them as animals. The sight and sound of them filled her with terror. It was as if the whole group of kids had gone insane, turning into mindless creatures who wanted nothing more than to win the bizarre game they were now playing. She felt like she was being hunted. *You* are *being hunted*, she reminded herself. But why?

At least she was starting to think like a boar. That was some help. At first she had just run blindly, taking whatever turn was available. But that had been a human way of thinking, and the "dogs" had caught on quickly. They'd been able to follow her easily, and once they'd almost gotten her when she'd turned too suddenly and slipped. But at the last moment she'd been able to get to her feet and keep one step ahead of them, narrowly missing being caught by the fingers of a girl who lunged out of nowhere.

Now she was thinking more clearly, trying to devise a strategy. Clearly the point of the game was to not get caught. But there had to be more to it than that. When was it over? Was there some target she was supposed to reach, like the "safe" tree in a game of tag? She didn't know what the rules of the hunt were, except that she had to stay one step ahead of Spider and the hounds. Until she had a better idea of what she was supposed to do, that's what she would concentrate on. But she needed a plan. What would a boar do? She had no idea.

You're thinking too hard, a voice in her head said. *Become the creature of the woods*. Cooper wanted to scream, "I already *am* a creature of the woods!" Instead, she tried to do what the voice said. She stopped thinking like herself and tried to become a boar. She imagined that it was all one big meditation exercise, and she allowed the boar's mind to take over. She could almost feel it happening. It was like a heavy curtain was drawn over the part of her brain that analyzed everything.

At the same time another curtain went up, and she found herself seeing the world around her in a totally new way. Her eyes saw patterns in the forest, and the trees became a maze that she was navigating. Her nose picked up scents she had ignored before, and she knew from smelling the air that there was water to her right. Something told her to stay away from the wet places, and she listened to it, turning left and running into a thick stand of trees.

"This one is smart, my hounds," she heard Spider cry out as his "dogs" tried to follow her and became caught up in the closely packed trees. "She is giving us more of a chase than I expected."

Cooper's human mind heard the hunter's words and felt a sense of pride. She was making the pack of wild kids look ridiculous. She was beating them at their own game. Then the boar part of her heard them and ran harder, desperate to put more distance between herself and the hounds. The "dogs" would find a way around the trees and be on her trail again soon. She couldn't rest. She had to keep moving.

"Boar," she heard someone call out in a loud whisper. "Boar. This way. Come this way."

Who was talking to her? She wanted to stop and look for the source of the voice, but she was afraid that it was some kind of trick. Probably one of the pursuers was trying to break her concentration and lure her into a trap. Well, she wasn't going to fall for it. Turning away from the voice, she began to run in a different direction.

"Don't worry, Boar," the voice said again. "I am a friend."

This time Cooper did stop. She was panting from having run so hard and so long, and her sides heaved in and out as she gulped in air. Somehow she had managed to lose the hunters for a moment. She heard them running through the trees some distance off, barking and sometimes laughing as they looked for her.

She looked around to see who had spoken to her and saw someone motioning to her from behind a tree. It was difficult to see who it was, so she crept closer, ready to run if it should be Spider or one of his gang. But it wasn't any of them—it was Bird.

"What are you doing?" Cooper asked. Of all of them, she was probably most angry at Bird. After all, she would never have been in this situation at all if she hadn't trusted Bird and gone with her.

"This way," Bird said.

Bird darted into the trees, her pale skin a ghostly shadow as it dipped beneath the branches. Cooper didn't know if Bird could be trusted. She'd led Cooper into trouble once already. Why would she want to see Cooper outwit Spider and the others after basically handing Cooper over to them in the first place? Cooper didn't let people make a fool of her more than once, and Bird had already used up her chance. But what other choice did Cooper have? She could keep running, but she still didn't know where she was going or what the point of the hunt was. Maybe Bird did. For whatever reason, she seemed to want to help Cooper now. Cooper hated having to depend on someone else to help her, but this time it looked like she didn't have any other real options. She ran after the other girl, keeping Bird in her sight as she darted along a few paces behind.

Bird seemed to know where she was going, and Cooper was happy to let her lead. The barking of the "dogs" grew more and more faint as they journeyed through the woods, and soon the sound of them faded away altogether. Bird slowed down, and Cooper was able to run a little more slowly. When Bird ducked beneath some trees and seemed to vanish, Cooper followed and found herself in a tiny glade completely ringed by trees and hidden from view.

"They won't find you here," Bird said, sitting on the ground. "At least not for some time."

"Why are they doing this?" asked Cooper, wanting to get as many answers as quickly as she could. She was exhausted, and she collapsed on the soft pine needles that blanketed the floor.

"They think it's fun," Bird said, sounding embarrassed. "Every Midsummer the Wild Hunt comes in search of the Midsummer boar. They have to find someone to be that boar. I guess you could say it's their sport. They don't mean any harm by it."

"That's really twisted," Cooper said. "They put

someone in the woods and then chase them around for fun? What's the point?"

"It's a kind of initiation," Bird said. "If you win, you get to be part of the group."

"Some prize," Cooper said. "Who would want to be part of a bunch of crazies like that?"

"I did," Bird said. "At least once. Now I'm not sure."

"You were the one who had to find the boar this year, weren't you?" Cooper said.

Bird nodded. "It's all part of the ritual," she said.

Now Cooper was beginning to understand. She still had a lot of unanswered questions that she wanted to put to Bird, but there wasn't time. Instead, she asked the one big one that was on her mind. "So how do I get out of this?"

"You have to escape the Wild Hunt," Bird said.

"I sort of got that part," Cooper asked. "It's the how I do that part I need to figure out. And what happens if I don't?"

"If you are captured by the hunt then Herne gains the prize he desires more than any other."

"Which is?" asked Cooper. She thought it was weird that even Bird referred to Spider by his make-believe name.

"The hand of Maeve, the Faerie Queen," said Bird.

"You mean, I'm some kind of trophy?" said Cooper. She couldn't believe that the weird hunt ritual was somehow connected to the larger one.

Did the organizers of the event really know that some of their participants were chasing a girl through the woods?

"I guess that's one way of looking at it," said Bird.

"How long do I have?" Cooper asked.

"Until midnight," said Bird. "When the shortest night is over, then the game is ended."

"You mean, I have to get chased by that pack of freaks until midnight?" said Cooper. She didn't know if she could do it. She was already exhausted, and surely Spider and the Wild Hunt would track her down sooner or later.

"There is one other way," said Bird. "The Wild Man has the power to end the game. He has in his possession something that belongs to you—a talisman. It was taken from you when you entered the woods with him. If you find where he has hidden it before you are caught, the magic will be ended."

"A talisman?" said Cooper. She tried to think what of hers might have been taken. She hadn't really brought anything with her on her journey except for the clothes she was wearing, and now those were gone. She hadn't brought anything else.

Except her flute. What had she done with it? She remembered putting it down when the Wild Man had told her to get into the stream. She remembered laying it on some leaves. He must have taken it when she was looking at her reflection in the water. He'd disappeared shortly after. He must have run away to hide it.

But where was it? That was what she had to figure out. If she could find the Wild Man and figure out what he had done with her flute, she could win the game and the horrible ordeal would be over. Now that she knew there was a way, she was more determined than ever to beat Spider and his friends at their game.

"I need to find my flute," Cooper told Bird. "That's what the Wild Man took. How do I find it?"

"To find it you must find him," Bird explained. "And that will not be easy. He will have hidden himself. But I think I may know where. We must go back into the woods to find him."

"You're sure this is the only way?" Cooper asked. "I can't just sit here and wait for midnight to roll around?"

Bird shook her head. "If midnight comes and neither side has won, the game is considered a draw," she said.

Cooper thought about that. It was an easy way out. She could just try to stay away from Spider and the others until then. But she didn't want that. She wanted to win. She wanted to show them that she could beat them.

"Listen," said Bird. "Already the hounds are coming."

Cooper perked up her ears and listened. Sure enough, she could hear the "dogs" in the distance. They had picked up her scent and were coming her way.

"Okay," she said. "Let's go find that flute."

She and Bird left the hiding place. Bird ran ahead, making sure there were no "dogs" lying in wait for them, and then Cooper followed. She had no idea where to look for the hidden talisman, but Bird seemed to.

Cooper followed Bird as she darted through the forest. It was very dark now, but there were patches of moonshine, and she could see Bird's shadows from time to time, and this kept her on course.

Unfortunately, the hounds of the Wild Hunt also seemed to be back on course. She heard them coming again, and now they appeared to be on all sides of her. From time to time one of them would let out a howl of excitement, and the sound chilled her blood. She almost forgot that they were just human guys and girls. In her imagination, they were Herne's hounds, doing his bidding and trying to track her down. They wanted her. Spider wanted her as his prize. What would he do with her if he caught her? she wondered.

"Are we almost there?" she asked Bird, panting with the exertion of trying to run and talk at the same time.

"I believe so," said Bird. "If I'm right, the hiding place is somewhere up ahead."

Cooper doubled her efforts, putting all the strength she had into getting away. The hounds were coming. They were running uphill. The ground rose sharply, and Cooper began having trouble keeping up her speed. Her heart was beating wildly, and all she wanted to do was stop. But Bird was moving quickly, and Cooper was determined to stay with her.

"It's here!" Bird said. "Just ahead. The place of hiding."

Cooper could hear the panting of the hounds behind her. Then she heard Spider cry out to them. "Now we have her!" She didn't have a lot of time left.

"Where is it?" she cried out. "Where is the talisman?"

They had reached the top of the hill that they'd been climbing. Cooper could see the line of black sky where the trees ended at the top. They were almost there. But so were the "dogs" and Spider. For a moment she felt the cold grip of fear around her heart. Had Bird tricked her? Was she really in on the game after all? Cooper almost turned and ran away, but the only thing waiting for her in the darkness was the hounds.

Bird was just ahead of her. She had stopped running and was standing still. Was she showing Cooper where the Wild Man had hidden the flute? Cooper raced up to Bird and stopped herself just before she ran headlong over the edge of an embankment. Standing on the edge, she could see the gleam of water below them.

"What is this?" she said, frightened. "You tricked me!"

"No," said Bird. "The Wild Man has gone down below. There is a deep pool there. And in the pool is where he has hidden your flute."

"In the water?" Cooper said, dismayed. "How am I supposed to get there?"

"There is only one way," said Bird. "The pool is ringed on all sides by banks such as these. The only way to reach it from here is to jump."

"*Jump* into it?" Cooper said. "Are you crazy?"

"It is the only way," Bird told her.

Cooper looked down at the pool. It seemed miles away. There was no way she was jumping from the cliff into it. There had to be another way. There just had to.

She heard panting and turned to see the hounds advancing on her. They moved slowly, their wild hair even more tangled than before, their eyes ringed with mud and their clothes torn and covered with leaves. With them came Spider.

"At last," he said, grinning as he walked toward Cooper. "The Midsummer boar is mine. It looks as if you've lost."

Cooper looked at Spider. He looked so sure of himself. The girls and guys gathered around him smirked at her. They knew they had her. They looked, too, at Bird, and for a moment Cooper wondered what they would do to her for helping Cooper try to outrun them.

"Are you ready to admit your defeat?" Spider asked Cooper.

Cooper looked into his face. She knew that he thought it was all over. He expected her to give in, to admit that she hadn't been clever enough to figure out the game and win it. That made her furious. No one treated her that way.

She turned and looked once more at the distant waters of the pool. The Wild Man was hidden down there somewhere, and so was her flute. If she retrieved it she would be set free. If she survived the jump. It looked like a long way away, although it was probably only twenty feet or so. Was it worth finding out?

The first hound lunged at her, trying to grab her wrist. She turned away, kicking at the boy with her foot. But she knew she didn't stand a chance. Her back was to the cliff, and there was no way out.

"You put up a good fight," Spider said. "But you're no match for us."

Cooper fixed him with a glare. "That's what you think," she said.

She turned and leapt from the high bank. For a moment she hung in space, the night sky filled with stars above her and blackness below her. Then she was rushing downward, the pool coming closer and closer.

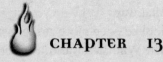 **CHAPTER 13**

The Holly King walked slowly through the woods, saying very little. He seemed to be looking at everything closely, as if he'd never seen it before.

"It always fascinates me how the woods change from one year to the next," he said when he and Annie had been walking for five or ten minutes. "These trees have grown quite tall since I was last here."

Annie made a noncommittal grunting sound. She still wasn't entirely comfortable about walking with the Holly King. She missed the comforting presence of the Oak King, and the new king's demeanor puzzled her. How could he act as if nothing had happened? Even in a game of pretend, shouldn't he at least feel *some* sadness about his brother's death, particularly since he himself had caused it? Instead, he was acting as if they were simply taking a walk.

"You are grieving over my brother's death," the Holly King said.

"I don't understand what happened back there," Annie admitted. "I know this is all part of the Midsummer ritual, but I've never seen anything like that. I thought that witchcraft was all about doing good, not about killing. Why do you do such a horrible thing?"

"Our ritual is as old as this forest," the Holly King answered. "It is as old as the seasons, as old as the world, as old as time. Many, many times my brother the Oak King and I have met on the field of battle and slain one another. It is the way of things."

"But why?" Annie asked persistently. "What's the point of it? Why can't you do some other kind of ritual?" She understood the reasons for performing ceremonies and rituals in general, but this one just didn't make any sense to her.

"There was a time," the Holly King explained, "when people offered up other lives to the land. Human lives. They did not fully understand the ways of the earth then, and they believed that only by offering up the blood of the best of them would the land bestow its gifts upon them. So they killed their kings, or others chosen to take the place of the kings."

Annie shuddered. What the Holly King was saying sounded terrible beyond words. She couldn't imagine people killing other people as sacrifices to the land. That was barbaric.

"Yes, it was cruel," the Holly King said. "But as I said, these people did not understand the earth.

They still thought that thunder and lightning were caused by the feet of cloud giants, and they believed that the sun was chased through the sky by a great wolf that devoured it every night. To them it made sense that they should give a precious gift to the earth, and what was more precious than the body and blood of their king?"

"What does all of this have to do with the ritual we just did?" asked Annie.

"My brother and I represent those sacrifices," the king told her. "No longer do people kill one another to appease an earth that doesn't require appeasing. My brother and I are willing sacrifices, each returning the other to the land and then rising again to rule for a time."

"Rising again?" Annie said. She still didn't get what the Holly King was saying to her.

"Tonight my brother was slain by my own hand," the Holly King said. "But he will rise again at Yule, when the year turns from waning back to waxing, when the sun is reborn of the Mother. On that night, when the night is longest, we will meet again in battle, and I will be the one who is slain. I am the ruler of the waning year, when the light turns to darkness and summer to winter. But he rules over the time when the light grows strong and summer comes to the world."

"You mean, you came back to life tonight?" replied Annie. "I mean, metaphorically. I know you didn't *really* come back to life."

"Oh, but I did," the king responded. "Just this evening I awoke from my sleep and was greeted by those who watch over me, just as my brother will be watched over during the long nights of winter when my spirits of the cold are flying across the land."

The Holly King's speech was very poetic, but it was also a little too much for Annie to take in. The man playing the king was certainly getting into his role, but she was pretty sure she'd had enough of kings and killing for one evening. She was anxious to get back to camp, to her friends, and to the rest of the Midsummer gathering.

"What was it you wanted to show me?" she asked the king.

"It is just up here," the Holly King told her. "You should feel very honored. No mortal has been taken to this place since the days of Arthur. We hide it well from the eyes of the curious. But through your devotion to my brother, I believe you have earned the right to see it."

The king stopped, reached into his pocket, and pulled out a blindfold. "But I must ask you to put this on," he said.

Annie looked doubtfully at the blindfold. Why did she need to wear it, especially in the dark? Was this some kind of trick? She didn't feel like she was in any danger, but she wasn't sure that the king wouldn't try to make a fool out of her as part of the Midsummer fun.

"I cannot take you where I wish to if you do not

put this on," he said. "But I assure you that I mean you no harm."

"Okay," Annie said unenthusiastically. She took the blindfold from the king and placed it over her eyes, tying it in a knot behind her head. Between its blinding effects and the surrounding darkness, she couldn't see anything at all. Even the light from the Holly King's torch was nothing but a vague blur.

The king took her hand and led her forward. "Don't worry," he said. "I won't let you fall."

Annie had no idea where they were going. They were walking upward, she knew that, but she didn't have any sense of what direction they were heading in. All she felt was the ground beneath her feet every time she took a step and the brushing of the branches against her skin as they passed by the trees. Then, after about five minutes, the king stopped. She heard what sounded like a door being opened, and then they were moving forward again. This time they were going down. She reached out with her foot and felt empty air.

"You are on a stairway," the Holly King informed her. "Wait one moment while I remove your blindfold."

He reached behind Annie and worked the knot loose. When the blindfold came off, Annie saw that they were indeed on a stairway. It was roughly carved out of solid stone, and it went down in a spiral. Behind them was a stone door that was shut. She wondered what it looked like from the outside, and how the stairs had come to be in the woods. Probably they were in some kind of abandoned water station or even an old bomb shelter from the days when people actually worried about things like that. She'd read a little bit about the shelters built in the woods around Beecher Falls, but she'd never seen one. Maybe the organizers of the ritual had gotten permission to use one for their activities.

However it had come to be there, Annie found it interesting. There were torches set into brackets in the walls every couple of yards, so she was able to see clearly as they descended the stairs. But she had no idea what awaited her at the bottom. For all she knew, they were just going to end up in an empty room. But she was curious, so she walked quickly with the Holly King behind her. When they reached the bottom of the stairs they were in a long hallway with a door at the opposite end.

"In there," said the Holly King, pointing to the door.

They walked to the small wooden door and the king pushed it open. Annie stepped through and found herself in a small vaulted chamber about the size of her bedroom. In the middle of the room was a raised stone platform, and on the platform lay the Oak King. He was resting on a bed of leaves and flowers, all of which looked as fresh and perfect as when they'd first been picked. His hands were still crossed over his chest, but his clothing had been changed and he was wearing clean robes of pale yellow.

The six attendants who had carried the king from the field stood around the platform, gazing down on their master attentively. When they heard the door open they turned and looked at the Holly King and Annie.

"She is permitted by my asking," the king said, and the attendants turned back to their fallen lord.

Annie walked over to the platform and looked down on the Oak King. His face was handsome, and he appeared to be at rest, his chest rising and falling with his breathing.

So he isn't really dead, she thought. Even though she knew the whole thing was a play, she'd still been a little worried. But now she felt better.

"Here he will lie for six months," the Holly King said, standing beside her. "And when he awakes at Yule, his attendants will help him rise and prepare him to come bring about my death."

"Why are you showing me this?" Annie asked. Apart from being sort of interesting to see, this part of the ritual didn't really make a lot of sense to her.

"I sense that you fear death," the Holly King said. "My brother chose you as his squire for a reason. I think he wanted you to see his death and to learn from it."

"He didn't choose me," Annie said stubbornly. "It was an accident. I ran into this guy in a fox mask who gave me a letter you wrote telling the Oak King to come meet you."

The Holly King laughed. "My brother needed no letter," he said. "And your coming to him was no accident. Most likely the fox was one of his own. But no matter. Now you are here, and now you see that even in death there is life."

That was the second time that night someone had said that to her. The Oak King had talked about death being part of life, too. It had irritated Annie then, and it irritated her now.

"Why do people keep saying that?" she said. "Is this some kind of get-Annie-to-deal-with-death day or something? Everywhere I go it's death this and death that. What happened to having a good time on Midsummer?"

"But there is much joy in Midsummer," the king said. "Even the death of the Oak King is cause for celebration because it means that the Wheel of the Year has turned yet again. Why must that bring sadness?"

"Because death sucks!" Annie shouted, suddenly overcome with anger. "Do you even know what a real death is like? You're just playing at this, putting on costumes and pretending to kill one another because you think it's really cool. But dying isn't cool. It's scary, and it hurts, and no one should have to do it."

She was breathing hard, glaring at the Holly King. Then she turned her attention to the sleeping

Oak King. "Get up!" she yelled. "Open your eyes! The game is over. I got it, all right? Death is this great big sacrifice that we're all supposed to be happy about. You can stop pretending to be dead now. I got your point."

The Oak King continued to remain motionless. Enraged, Annie ran over and began to beat on his chest. "Get up!" she shouted. "Get up, get up, get up!"

When the king still refused to move, she began to cry. Tears fell from her eyes onto his yellow robes, staining the silk. Why wouldn't he open his eyes and end the horrible game? Why were they making her do this? It was cruel. Whoever had devised this little "surprise" for her was going to get an earful when she found out who it was.

"I want you to wake up!" she said, grabbing the Oak King by the collar of his robe and trying to shake him. The attendants ran over and began to pull her away, but she fought against them, pushing their hands off and venting her fury and sadness on the unresponsive figure on the stone platform.

"Let her be," the Holly King ordered, and the Oak King's watchers released her. She ran back to him and threw herself across his body.

"Please," she said, her screams of rage becoming softer. "Please don't do this anymore. I don't want to go through this again. I don't want to lose you again. Please, Daddy, wake up."

She had become a little girl of six, calling for the father who had left her. In her heart she knew that the Oak King wasn't her father. But he had re-minded her so much of him. She hadn't realized that until now, hadn't realized how watching him die had been like reliving that long-ago night over again as if it was all being played out in horrible, vivid detail.

Now that she did, she cried even more. She had never really cried for her father and her mother. She'd been told to be brave, and she thought that meant keeping all of the hurt she felt inside. That's why she didn't talk about it very much. She didn't want to bring it back to life, to risk opening up the wounds that had scarred over during years of being brave.

"Daddy," she said again, the word sounding unfamiliar to her after not saying it for so long. "Daddy." She wanted to say something—anything—else, but it was as if now that she'd started she couldn't stop, couldn't say anything but that one word. She was afraid that the man playing the Oak King must think she had gone crazy, but she couldn't help it. The experiences of the evening had brought up all kinds of emotions in her, and they were all trying to come out at once.

Suddenly she felt someone grab her hand. She looked down and saw that one of the Oak King's hands was holding hers tightly. His fingers clasped hers gently but firmly. Surprised, she looked at his face. His eyes were open, and he was smiling.

"Little hedgehog," he said. "You have stirred me

from my sleep. I have come only to tell you that the waning year holds much for you. Do not be afraid of what you will see and experience. This night has prepared you for it."

The Oak King opened his arms. He pulled Annie to him and held her. As he did, she felt something inside her break open and she began to sob uncontrollably.

"There, there, little hedgehog," the Oak King said. "It was just a game. Now it's over. There's no need to weep."

"I thought you might really be dead," Annie said, feeling very foolish but unable to stop herself. "I thought you were dead just like they are."

"You mean your parents?" the king said.

Annie nodded. The king released her, and she stepped away from him, rubbing the tears from her face. She looked at the Holly King and then back at the Oak King, who looked at her kindly.

"Would you like to tell me what happened?" the Oak King said.

Annie nodded. For the first time since the accident she was ready to talk. It was time.

CHAPTER 14

"Where are we going?" Kate asked the two children. They seemed to be leading her away from the main ritual area, and that bothered her. Maybe they *were* part of whatever game she was playing, but maybe they were just as lost as she was. After all, how old could they be? Eight? Nine? And she still thought it was odd that they were running around in the woods alone so late at night. It had to be after eleven.

"Hey, do you two even know where you're going?" she tried again. "I hope your parents are around here somewhere."

The children laughed, but they didn't say anything to her. It was as if they were teasing her, drawing her deeper and deeper into the forest. But she kept following them, hoping that eventually they would take her somewhere close to where she wanted to be.

Just as she was tiring of being pulled through branches in the dark, the woods opened up and she found that they were standing on the shores of the lake. The children stopped at the edge of the water and waited for Kate to catch up with them.

"There," they said, pointing into the middle of the water.

Kate looked and saw that they were indicating the island that sat in the middle of the lake. The moon hung directly above it, bathing it in silver light, and it looked almost like a spaceship had landed and was floating on the water.

"What's going on here?" she asked the little girl and boy.

"Come," they said, walking toward the water.

Then Kate saw that there was a boat pulled up onto the beach. It was a rowboat, painted white, and its bow was decorated with a wreath of roses. The children pushed against it, shoving it into the water. The little girl turned and beckoned to Kate with one finger.

When she reached the shore, Kate stepped gently into the rowboat, feeling it rock beneath her weight. The floor was strewn with rose petals, and she was surrounded by a wonderful smell as she took her seat and faced the island. The little girl and boy gave one final push, and Kate found herself floating out into the lake as they remained on-shore.

"Hey!" she called out. "What's going on?"

Then she saw the oars resting in the boat's oar-locks. Grabbing them, she began trying to turn the boat around. Then she looked at the island and decided that maybe she should see what was waiting out there. After all, everything had led her here. She might as well see the game out to the end.

Slowly but steadily, the boat made for the island. The closer she got, Kate saw that the entire island was covered in different colored lights. They twinkled merrily, blinking on and off like faeries flitting from one branch to the next. But before she had time to wonder how it had all been done, the boat was scraping the shore. Kate climbed out and pulled the little craft up to the beach.

But what was she supposed to do now? There was no one on the shore, and Kate didn't know where to go. Then she noticed that to her right the lights formed a sort of doorway leading into the trees. Was she supposed to go through it? It seemed the likeliest choice. She walked to the doorway and stepped through.

She found herself on a path that wound in and out of the trees as she followed it. The branches around her were filled with the same blinking lights she'd seen from the shore, and she tried to see what was making the beautiful glow. But none of the lights stayed lit long enough for her to discern the source. As soon as she moved in for a closer look they went out and reappeared somewhere else.

It must be fireflies again, she thought. *But do they flash in color?* She didn't think they did.

The path ended abruptly as the trees opened up into a large clearing. Kate ran into it and stopped. The moon hung right overhead, filling it with light that seemed brighter than it could possibly be. It was almost like twilight in the circle, and what the light illuminated was stranger than anything Kate had ever seen.

A group of people ringed the clearing, a group unlike anything Kate had set her eyes on before. Some were definitely human, or at least human-looking. But they were unnaturally beautiful. Their eyes sparkled even in the darkness. Their faces looked as if they'd been formed by the most skilled craftsmen. And their clothes were gorgeous, made of material that sparkled and shimmered like water when they moved.

Others were definitely not human, at least not entirely. There were creatures with the bodies of women and men but the heads of stags or bears or rabbits. They stood talking to one another in quiet voices and looking at the newcomer. And all around them flew the peculiar lights, bathing them in a kaleidoscope of ever-changing color.

What amazing costumes, Kate thought. She looked down at her own dress. It was dirty and torn from her night in the woods. The wings at her back hung forlornly to one side. She knew she looked terrible. This wasn't how she'd wanted to make her entrance at the big Midsummer dance. She assumed that that's where she was. It was a clever trick, telling them that the dance would be in the main clearing and then moving it to this place. How many other people had been fooled?

She looked around for familiar faces. Were Annie and Cooper there? Was Tyler? She was anxious to see them and find out what had been happening to them all night. Well, except maybe for Tyler. She'd started off the evening being happy to be with him. Now she wasn't sure how she felt about anything.

"I see you've come," a voice said, making her look up.

It was Maeve. As she entered the circle, the people around her stood back. Kate could see why. She looked even more beautiful than she had the other times Kate had seen her. She was dressed in a pink-and-white gown that sparkled with tiny lights. Her black hair fell around her face in curls. She looked magnificent.

"Yes," Kate said. "I made it. Although my costume could use some help."

"That doesn't matter," the queen told her. "What matters is that you followed your heart here. Do you remember what I asked you earlier tonight?"

"About my greatest desire?" Kate said. "I told you it was true love. But I think I should have said something else. The whole love thing didn't really work out."

"The night is not yet over," Maeve told her.

"I think maybe I should stick with dancing," Kate told her. "It's easier."

"There will be dancing soon," said the Faerie Queen. "But first you must finish your quest."

Kate didn't understand. Hadn't Maeve been listening? She'd lost Tyler in the woods somewhere. She'd run away from Scott. And most of the time she'd been walking around with a guy dressed as a faun. As far as romance went, this was about the least romantic evening she'd ever spent in her life.

"Very few are invited to my island," said Maeve, sounding annoyed. "Are you refusing my challenge?"

There was murmuring among the crowd as the queen stared at Kate. Kate didn't know what to say. Why was she being singled out like this? Why weren't the others being put in the spotlight? Was someone trying to make her look like a fool? She looked around the circle, trying to figure out who would do such a thing. But all the faces were either unrecognizable or hidden behind masks.

"What do I have to do?" she asked impatiently. She just wanted to get the thing over with so the dance could start.

"You must choose," Maeve said.

"Choose?" Kate repeated, not understanding.

"Your lover," Maeve told her. "It is time to choose your lover."

Kate was confused. What was the queen talking about? How could she choose her lover? Before she could ask, Maeve lifted a hand. The crowd behind her parted and Kate saw some figures being led into the ring. The first person she saw was Tyler. He was still wearing the raven mask, and he was being led by a man with a bear head. The sight of Tyler was unnerving, but not nearly as unnerving as what Kate saw next. Behind Tyler came a woman whose long blond hair hung in three braids down her back. And walking behind her was Scott.

Kate wanted to die. What was Scott doing there? It was bad enough that she had run into him in the woods. But now he was being paraded in front of her Wiccan friends. Worse, he was in the same place that Tyler was. How had Maeve found out about him, and how had she convinced him to take part in whatever weird joke they were playing on Kate?

She was furious. She didn't mind going along with some games as part of a Midsummer ritual. That was half the fun of celebrating the sabbats. But this was too much. Now her private life was being dragged into things, and she didn't like that at all.

"What's going on?" she demanded angrily. "Who did this?"

Maeve looked at her with a curious expression. "Did you not tell me that you wanted to find your true love?" she asked. "I'm giving you the chance."

She turned and indicated the two guys, who stood side by side in the middle of the clearing with the crowd gathered around them. Kate looked at each of them. Tyler was peering nervously around.

Scott just looked confused, as if he wasn't sure how he'd gotten there.

"All you have to do is choose," the Faerie Queen said. "But you must choose correctly."

"Or else what?" asked Kate.

"Or else all of you will remain here with me forever," the queen told her.

Hearing this, Tyler and Scott looked up. *They almost seem frightened*, Kate thought. But surely they must know that it was all a game. At least, Tyler should know. Scott, on the other hand, had good reason to be confused. Kate hoped he would believe it was all just part of the costume party she'd told him she was going to. But even if he did, she was going to have a lot of explaining to do.

"Well then," Kate said, deciding that if she was going to be made a fool of she was going to give as good as she got, "I suppose I'd better pick the right one. I wouldn't want to have to live in this dress for the rest of my life."

Maeve frowned, and there was a collective gasp from the crowd. *Oh, grow up*, Kate thought. *This is just a stupid game*.

"You get only one chance," Maeve said. "Look at both carefully before you pick. When you have chosen, you must give the other a kiss good-bye. The one who remains will be your true love."

Kate walked confidently into the center of the ring. How hard could this be? She knew who she was going to pick. Even if she was mad at Tyler, he was still her boyfriend. She certainly wasn't going to choose Scott.

She walked back and forth in front of the two guys. Although she knew who she was going to pick, she figured she might as well make things a little bit interesting for those who were watching. She pretended to study each face carefully, as if she really couldn't decide which one she wanted to call her lover.

Then, to her amazement, she found that she really *wasn't* as sure as she'd thought she was. The raven-masked guy had seemed the only choice. But as she looked at the two faces she found that she was reluctant to choose. She stopped in front of Scott and looked at him. He was so handsome, and they'd had some great times together. She'd wanted him for so long, and getting him for her own had been a dream come true. Breaking up with him had been awful, and several times she'd thought that maybe she'd made a mistake. Had she? Was he really the one for her after all?

She moved on and looked at Tyler. Even behind the raven mask, he was watching her intently, studying her every move. She'd left Scott for him because he'd made her feel as if she could be anyone she wanted to be. She didn't feel as if she had to live up to his idea of what a girlfriend should be, which Scott sometimes insisted she do. She could be herself. She could talk about Wicca with him, which she never could do with Scott.

She looked from Scott to Tyler. Each one had good points. But each one had bad points, too. Scott was caught up in being popular and fitting in. That meant that Kate had to hide part of who she was with him. And although Tyler had always seemed to be a perfect boyfriend, tonight he had really disappointed her by running off and leaving her to walk around in the woods by herself. Even if it was just a game, she'd hoped that he would be more caring than that. And now he was letting her be embarrassed in front of the others. That wasn't the Tyler she thought she knew.

Still, when she thought about it she knew that she really did love Tyler. But maybe she should embarrass him by choosing Scott. That would serve him right. After all, this was just pretend. She could have her fun, make Tyler see how upset she was with him, and then make up later. Of course, getting rid of Scott would be another problem, but she could worry about that later.

"It is time to choose," the queen said. "Select the loser."

Kate looked at the two faces. Who should she pick? Did she really want to embarrass Tyler? Part of her did. It would serve him right. But another part wanted him to know that she loved him even when he acted like a jerk. *Maybe you've learned something from all of this after all*, she thought as she gave one last long look at both of them and made up her mind.

"I have chosen," said Kate. She stood in front of Tyler and Scott.

"My true love is many things," she said to the crowd. "He is kind and gentle. He is brave. He loves me when I look good and when I look not so good. He helps me when I need help."

She looked from Tyler to Scott. Tyler's bird face was turned to one side, watching her. Scott was looking at her expectantly. She walked over to Scott.

"There's part of me that really likes being with you," she said. "But you're not my heart's desire."

Leaning up, she kissed Scott on the lips. He barely even moved. When she pulled away, he looked at her, stricken.

"But you kissed me that day on the beach," he said. "And again tonight."

Maeve lifted her hand. "Is this true?" she asked.

Kate looked at her, then at Tyler, who was staring at the ground. She wondered what he was thinking. She knew he was waiting to hear her answer. Should she lie, say that Scott was making everything up? Or should she admit what she'd done and pay whatever price came with it?

"Yes," she said finally. "It's true." She'd been keeping her Skip Day kiss with Scott a secret from Tyler for too long.

Maeve walked over and stood next to her. "An untrue heart is not worthy of true love," she said sternly.

"But I do love Tyler," Kate said. "I was just confused."

"Then how do I know you are telling the truth now?" asked Maeve. "Perhaps you are again confused."

"Kate," Scott said, his voice sadder than she'd ever heard it. "I don't know what all of this is. But I do know that I love you—and I think you love me. Please, choose me."

Kate looked at his hopeful face. "I'm sorry," she said.

"I am not convinced," Maeve said. "I need proof. Is there none here who will speak for this girl?"

Kate's heart seemed to stop as she waited for someone to say something. All around her the eyes of the costumed crowd were upon her, and she felt as if she were on trial. What would happen if no one helped her? She was already embarrassed enough. This just made it all much worse.

"I will speak for her," a voice said.

The crowd parted, and the faun walked into the clearing. There was murmuring at his appearance, and Maeve seemed slightly annoyed to see him.

"What have you to say about this?" she asked him.

The faun looked at Kate. "I tried to tempt this

girl," he said. "But she resisted. Her love is true."

Maeve glanced at Kate. "Very well, then," she said. "Go to your beloved."

There was a stirring in the crowd as Kate walked to the raven-faced boy and kissed him. The Faerie Queen clapped her hands.

"The girl has chosen correctly," she said. "Let her and her lover stay with us and dance."

Immediately the air was filled with the sound of music, and all around the circle people began to dance. Tyler and Kate were swept up in the excitement, and they found themselves moving around the ring hand in hand. Kate wanted to talk to Tyler, but there would be time for that later. She just wanted to enjoy herself for a while after everything she'd been through. She was so happy that she'd picked Tyler after all. But what had happened to Scott? She looked around and couldn't see him anywhere. Had he run off? She felt bad about hurting him, but she'd had to do it. She hoped that someday, somehow, he could understand that.

The music seemed to increase in tempo as they danced, and Kate was growing dizzy from moving so quickly. She needed to rest. But the hands on either side of her pulled her onward, around and around the circle. She couldn't stop. They were moving impossibly quickly. Where was Tyler? Was that his hand holding hers? She couldn't tell.

They seemed to dance forever. Kate looked up

at the sky and saw the moon looking down on them. Then it seemed to swirl around, becoming a blur, and she felt herself falling. She closed her eyes, trying to stop the dizziness, and then everything went black.

CHAPTER 15

Cooper hit the water with a splash. It was colder than she'd expected it to be, and the shock took her breath away. As she plunged downward, deeper and deeper, she was sure that she was going to slam against the bottom. Surely the pool couldn't be that deep. Any second she expected to feel a rock strike her head, and the rushing of the water in her ears disoriented her so that she didn't know which way was up. The water filled her nose and mouth, and she worried that even if she did survive the plunge from the cliff she would drown.

But she didn't hit any rocks, and she didn't drown. The pool seemed to be very deep. Eventually she stopped going down. Her body slowed, and she was able to kick her legs. Faint glimmers of light shone above her, and she pushed herself toward them. The bubbles coming from her nose swarmed around her like bees, and she followed them to the surface, her head breaking through just as she was sure that the last drops of oxygen in her lungs would give out.

She gulped air in great gasping breaths. She swam to the edge of the pool and scrambled onto the bank, relieved to be out of the water. She stood there, shaking the water from her hair and enjoying the feeling of being on solid land. Then she heard the angry howling of the "dogs" and she remembered the reason for her leap. Looking up, she saw the shapes of Spider and the others far above her, outlined in the moonlight. She had a feeling that they wouldn't jump after her. She had defied them, and she had escaped them. But the sight and sound of them still filled her with fear. She had come very close to becoming Spider's prize, and she didn't think she would ever forget how that felt. Even though she didn't think she'd been in any real danger, it had been a moment of absolute terror, so strong that she had overcome her fear of the cliff in order to save herself.

But she wasn't finished yet. She still had to find the flute that the Wild Man had stolen from her. If she didn't find it before midnight, the game would still be a draw and everything she and Bird had done would be for nothing. She didn't want that. She wanted to win everything. She wanted to prove to Spider, the others, and herself that she was stronger than anything they could throw at her.

But where was the Wild Man, and where exactly had he hidden the flute? Bird had said that he had hidden it somewhere in the pool. But the pool was so deep. How could she find it, especially in the dark? She couldn't see anything, and the flute could be anywhere.

She stared into the pool. Its black surface was smooth as glass. The moon reflected in it was high in the sky, and Cooper knew that it must be getting close to midnight. She didn't have a lot of time. She had to find the flute quickly.

"Where are you?" she shouted. "Come out. I've found your hiding place. Now show yourself."

There was no answer to her call. She looked up at the cliff and saw that Spider and his hounds had disappeared. For a moment she wondered if they'd taken Bird with them. But she didn't have time to worry about the girl. She had work to do.

She circled the pond, looking into it. She was growing more and more frustrated. She'd gotten this far, and now she didn't know how to proceed. It was like finding a treasure chest and discovering that it was locked and there was no key to open it. The flute was waiting for her. She needed to find it. But how?

She sat down at the edge of the pool and tried to quiet her mind. Using the meditation techniques she'd developed, she imagined herself in a quiet, safe place. She let herself relax as much as she could, and she tried to focus on the problem at hand.

But all she felt was the wind blowing on her

skin. Her clothes were still wet, and she was cold. She wished the wind would die down, but it continued to tease her, tickling her cheeks and rushing over her skin. Why wouldn't it leave her alone? It was like a fly buzzing in her ear, distracting her from what was important.

Or maybe it was giving her a clue. Suddenly she thought about wind, and fire, and the other elements that were so familiar to anyone who participated in Wiccan rituals. Earlier she had connected with the element of earth when she'd covered herself in mud and become a wild creature of the forest. Once before—when she'd had visions about a dead girl—she'd had to enter the realm of fire to solve the mystery that confronted her. Perhaps this test also involved becoming closer to one of the elements.

Water. She opened her eyes and looked at the pond. The water was black and cold and still. Somewhere in its depths lay her flute. In order to find it she would have to enter the realm of water again.

"What's with me and the elements?" she said aloud. Neither Annie nor Kate ever had to deal with obstacles like jumping into fires or covering themselves with mud. Why her?

Connections. The word popped into her head. She had survived so far because she had allowed herself to connect to different aspects of the natural world. In helping the dead girl, she had connected to fire and all that it represented. In escaping Spider and the hounds, she had connected to earth. *Connection* had been the word she'd drawn during the dedication ritual at which she'd promised to walk the Wiccan path for a year and a day. That was what her journey was supposed to be about, and that's what this particular journey had ended up being about as well.

Is that what this is? she asked herself. *Is this another part of my path?* She didn't like to think so. What had happened to her during the vision—what was still happening to her—was horrible. She had been put at great risk. Suddenly she found herself angry at those who had let this happen to her. If this is what working with magic and witchcraft resulted in, maybe it wasn't as wonderful as she'd thought, or as she'd been led to believe by her teachers.

She would have to think about that later. Right now she had a date with some water. She knew that's what she had to do—enter the realm of water again and somehow connect with it in order to fulfill her final task. She didn't like it, any more than she'd liked going into the fire, but she knew it was the way through.

She stood up and looked into the pond. "Okay," she said. "Here goes nothing."

Taking a deep breath, she jumped once more into the cold water. As she plunged into it, she felt the shock of it fill her completely. The first time it had been so quick and fierce that she hadn't had time to really feel it. Now she did. She let it soak into her skin and into her bones.

She turned and pointed her head downward. Kicking, she dove into the blackness. She kept her eyes shut, knowing that having them open wouldn't help anyway. She just swam, her hands pulling her deeper and deeper as she tried to conserve the air in her lungs. She tried to feel the water as if it were her home. She pretended she was a fish, the same way she'd pretended to be a boar.

"Okay, water," she said. "Do your stuff."

Deeper and deeper she went. She could feel the water grow colder as she went down. She also felt the air she'd drawn in before diving start to run out. She didn't know how much farther she could go before she would have to turn around. But she had to find the flute. She knew it was there, waiting for her.

Then her hand touched rock. She'd reached the bottom. *How deep am I?* she wondered. She tried not to think about whether she had enough air to get back to the surface.

Her hands moved over the bottom of the pool, finding rocks and some plants but little else. Was the flute even there? She had no way of knowing. Nor did she know how wide the pool bottom was.

She calmed her thoughts and let herself relax in the water. Her body floated, and she felt weightless. Was this what it felt like to drown? It was an odd sensation. She almost felt sleepy. The water rocked her gently in its arms, and even though she was cold and her lungs were starting to ache, she felt comforted.

Then her hands touched something. It felt almost like a stick, but harder. Her fingers scrambled along the length, and she felt the small familiar keys of her flute. She'd found it. Quickly, she snatched it up and turned her head back to the surface.

Kicking hard, she raced for the top of the pool. Now that she had her prize, getting back up to the world of air was the most important thing she could imagine. Her feet beat the water as her hands pulled her up, and the water rushed in her ears. She was almost there. Her head broke the surface and she let out a shout of triumph. She'd done it.

"So you've won," a voice said.

Cooper looked up and saw the Wild Man standing at the edge of the pool, watching her. She swam over and climbed out.

"It looks that way," she said. "Now, show me the way out of here."

The Wild Man pointed a finger away from the pond. "There is a path there," he said. "Follow it and you will leave this place and return to your own. But be warned—the faeries will not want you to go."

"Thanks for the warning," Cooper said, glad he was finally talking but annoyed that he still insisted on pretending they were playing with some kind of faerie magic instead of a bunch of crazy teenagers. "I think I can handle them."

She walked in the direction the Wild Man had pointed in. Sure enough, she found that a narrow path led away from the pool. It passed between the cliff walls and was just big enough for her to slip through. She was walking through a tunnel beneath the mountains. It was dark, but she kept going. Then she saw a pale light ahead of her. She walked toward it, hoping it was a way out, and soon she found herself surrounded by a purple fog that filled her eyes.

She waved the fog away, and when it cleared she saw that she was in the cave again. The fire was still burning in the center of the room, and Spider was sitting on one side of it.

"Welcome back," Spider said. "Did you enjoy the adventure?"

"Next time I'll pick Disneyland," Cooper said testily. "Just what did you think you were doing?"

Spider cocked his head. "Didn't you like our little game?" he asked.

"Not much," Cooper said. "I don't know who you people are, but trust me—you're going to be in it but deep when I find Sophia and the others."

Spider laughed. "It was just a little fun," he said. "An initiation of sorts. You said yourself that you were looking forward to your initiation."

"What you did was more like fraternity hazing," Cooper said. "Now, get out of my way. I want to get out of here."

She stood up and started for the exit. Spider rose as well. "Wait," he said. "We're not finished."

Cooper turned and looked at him. "Oh, I think we are," she said.

Spider smiled. "But what about your prize?" he said.

Cooper looked at him blankly.

"Have you forgotten?" he said. "You passed the test. You met your challenge by entering the Cave of Visions and completing your journey. Now you may play with us."

"Oh, that," said Cooper, smacking her forehead in a sarcastic gesture. "You know what—I think I'll skip it. I'm really tired, and it's got to be almost midnight. I'm just going to go find the others."

"But we want you in our group," Spider said. "You have proven yourself worthy."

All of a sudden the other members of the group came filing into the cave. They formed a ring around Cooper. They were holding their instruments in their hands, and their dirty faces stared at her.

"Please," said Spider. "Play with us."

Cooper looked at the kids surrounding her. Bird was among them, looking very unhappy. She saw Bird looking at her, a strange expression on her face. Suddenly she wanted to be out of the cave and away from the whole bunch of them.

"Look, I think you guys did a great job with this whole thing," Cooper said. "At least, for a bunch of lunatics. But I've had enough. Right now I want to leave."

"I'm afraid we can't allow that," Spider said. His voice no longer sounded friendly. It sounded cruel. Cooper turned and looked at him.

"I don't really care what you think about it," she said, her anger rising. "I'm leaving."

"I don't think Bird would like that, would you, Bird?" said Spider.

Cooper looked at Bird. The other girl looked away.

"What's going on here?" Cooper demanded. "Who are you people?"

The others laughed. "Haven't you guessed by now?" Spider said. "I would think one who could escape from the Wild Hunt would be more clever than that."

"Let me guess," she said. "You're supposed to be faeries."

There was more laughter from the others. Spider smiled. "Very good," he said.

Cooper wheeled around and stared hard at Bird. "You too?" she asked. "Are you still playing their little game, or are you going to stand up to them?"

Spider laughed loudly. "Oh, no. Bird is not a faerie. She is a mortal, like you. She came to us many years ago, drawn by our music, as you were."

"Oh, is that so?" Cooper asked.

"Yes," Spider said. "But now Bird has tired of us. We told her that if she found one to replace her she might go. She played and you came to her. You passed the test. Now it is your turn to play with our merry band."

"You people are nuts," Cooper said. She couldn't believe the ridiculous story they were telling her.

She started to push her way through to the entrance, but suddenly the cave filled with music as the others began to play their instruments. Almost immediately, Cooper felt her head fill with the intoxicating sounds that had first drawn her to Bird.

She spun around to tell them to stop, her hands over her ears as she tried to block the sounds of the music. But there was no way to get away from it. At the same time, the players began to dance around her, blocking the way out and making her lose her sense of direction.

"Stop it!" she yelled. "Stop!"

She fell to her knees, fighting the music. But it was too strong. The weird melody ran through her mind, calling to her, and she couldn't resist it. She wanted to play along with the weird faerie kids. She wanted to join them. Even after what they'd done to her. And that made her madder than anything else.

The music of the players swept over Cooper. She knew what Spider and the rest said about being faeries was pure make-believe. The people moving around her were just ordinary kids, like she was.

Someone broke from the dancing band and ran to her. It was Bird.

"Quickly," she said. "There's no time. Take my hand."

Cooper grabbed Bird's hand and was pulled through the swarm of musicians and out of the cave.

Once outside, Cooper didn't know what to say. Clearly, Bird was having some kind of reaction to the purple smoke or to the music or to what had happened during the night. Maybe she was still playing some kind of game.

Bird took Cooper's hand. "I couldn't let you take my place," she said.

Cooper's mind was spinning. "Let's get out of here," she said to Bird. "It's time to finish this."

"You go," Bird said. "My journey is over. I have been with the faeries too long. But you are safe from them now." With that, she turned and disappeared back into the cave.

"Bird!" Cooper called after her. "Bird!"

She didn't know what was wrong with Bird. If this was a game, it wasn't funny at all. She stood up and ran for the entrance.

But Bird was gone, and so were the rest. Where they had been, there was some oddly colored dust, but that was it. Where were they? They couldn't have just gotten up and left so quickly. *They must have run out the back*, Cooper thought. *It must be part of this crazy ritual.* Well, it was time for the ritual to end. She ran to the rear of the cave, determined to find Bird, Spider, and the rest of the faeries. But when she got there she found that she couldn't find either of the entrances she'd come through back into the cave.

She was furious. She'd been toyed with all night, first with Spider's game and now with this. She was through with all of it. If they wanted to laugh at her, that was fine with her. She turned and stormed out of the cave, slipping through the entrance and into the night. It was time to find Kate and Annie. She had a few things to tell them.

CHAPTER 16

"They were killed," Annie said before she could change her mind. "In a fire."

She hadn't told anyone about her parents or the fire, not even Cooper and Kate. In fact, she hadn't talked about the fire since the day almost ten years ago when her aunt had come to take her and Meg from their home in San Francisco to her house in Beecher Falls. Even thinking about it made Annie too sad; talking about it had always been impossible.

Now that she'd said the words out loud, though, she found that the fear that had always accompanied any thoughts of talking about the fire had lessened a little. Not much, but enough that she could at least voice the words.

"In a fire?" said the Oak King gently.

Annie nodded. Having told him the first part of what had always been one of her most closely guarded secrets, she found herself wanting to tell him more.

"It was my fault," she said quietly.

"Come now," said the king. "You're only a child. How could it have been your fault?"

"It was," Annie said insistently. "I started it." She had never told anyone any of this before, not even her aunt. She didn't know why she was saying any of it now. She'd always been so careful not to talk about it. But it was as if the words were flowing out before she could stop them.

"It was Christmastime," she said slowly, as if trying to remember all of the details so that she would get the story right. "I was six and Meg was just a baby. We had this beautiful tree all covered in lights. I liked to sit and look at it. I liked the way they twinkled on and off like stars."

Annie paused, not sure she could continue. The Oak King was watching her intently, not saying anything. She knew that he was waiting for her to go on. She took a breath.

"Every night when we went to bed my father made sure the tree was unplugged," she said. "But one night I wanted to see the lights, and I went downstairs in the middle of the night and plugged the tree in. I sat on the sofa and looked at them blinking on and off, and I fell asleep. When I woke up the room was filled with smoke."

She felt a tear slip from her eye and run down her cheek. She didn't bother to wipe it away, knowing that more were about to follow it.

"I shouted for my parents," Annie said. "I couldn't

see anything, and I couldn't breathe. I tried to run out of the room, but it was too hot and there was too much smoke. So I hid behind the sofa and screamed. The tree was on fire, and the fire was spreading to the rest of the room."

The tears were coming quickly now. The two kings were watching her, but she no longer felt ashamed of being sad.

"My father came into the room calling my name," she said. "I cried for help, and he found me. I remember him picking me up and running outside. I remember finally being able to breathe."

She stopped. She was reliving that night all over again in her memories. She really could smell the smoke from the fire and feel the heat of it on her skin. She recalled, too, the way she had felt so loved and safe in her father's arms when he carried her out of the house and told her to go stand in the garden until he came back.

Then she remembered how scared she was when he let go of her and ran back into the burning house. This was the part she didn't want to remember. But it was part of her story, and she had to tell it, no matter how painful it was. Gaining her composure, she started speaking again.

"My mother and Meg were still inside," she said. "My mother had gone upstairs to get Meg out of her crib. But I guess the smoke was too much for her, and she couldn't find her way out. My father ran back in, grabbed Meg, and brought her out to me.

He told me to hold her and to take care of her until he and my mother came back."

She couldn't say any more. The tears were streaming down her face now, and her voice had started to hitch. She knew that if she said another word she would start crying uncontrollably.

The Oak King came over and stood in front of Annie. "Your parents, they did not come out of the house, did they?"

Annie shook her head. "My father died trying to save my mother," she said before grief overcame her and she couldn't hold the tears back any longer. Her shoulders shook as she sobbed, letting it all out. "And it was all my fault."

She felt the Oak King's arms go around her, pulling her close once more. Normally, she would shy away from being held like that, believing that she should be able to control her emotions. But his touch was so caring, so gentle, that she didn't want him to let go. Several times during the night he had comforted her. Now she put her arms around him and buried her face in his chest, crying.

She hadn't cried that way since the neighbors, seeing the smoke and flames, had come out of their house and forced her and Meg out of the garden and away from the burning house. She had screamed at them then, trying to run back inside to find her father and mother. She had screamed while the fire trucks came and the firemen put out the blaze, beating at the man who was holding her and crying out for her mother or father to come out and make her feel better.

But they hadn't come out. After the flames were quenched and the trucks had gone away, she'd looked at the house and not understood why her parents didn't just walk out the front door. The outside of the house, while scorched, hid the horrible destruction within its walls. She was never allowed to see it. But she'd imagined it often enough in dreams since then—the blackened walls, the charred furniture, the ruined Christmas presents lying in filthy tatters on the floor.

And it was all because of you, she told herself for probably the six millionth time. Even though everyone from the firemen to her aunt had told her repeatedly that the fire was not her fault, she knew that wasn't true. She had plugged in the lights when she knew she wasn't supposed to and had fallen asleep with them on. She had been unable to find her way out. She had been the reason her father had to go back inside. But she had lived, and he had died along with her mother.

She felt like she was six years old again, and it felt horrible. She'd thought that maybe she'd started to make peace with her parents' deaths the month before, when her aunt had surprised her by organizing a showing of her mother's artwork. She'd also found a box of photographs of Annie, Meg, and their parents that Annie had never seen before. These things had all helped reconnect

Annie with her parents. But they hadn't helped her confront the one big thing that had haunted her ever since that night almost ten years ago. She'd kept that buried deep inside. But now it was out, and she had to face it.

The king continued to hold her as she cried. She was afraid that he was going to start saying all of the well-meaning things that people had said to her when the fire had occurred, like "It was an accident" and "You know your parents loved you very much." She'd heard those things over and over again, and they hadn't helped at all. Of course, it had been an accident. Of course, her parents had loved her. But that didn't change the fact that she had been responsible for their deaths.

"You need to remember," was what the Oak King said finally. "You need to remember what happened, and you need to remember your father and mother." His voice was calm and filled with great sadness. Annie wanted him to hold her forever. She hadn't felt so safe in years, not since her own father had held her. Thinking about that made her start crying all over again.

"I miss them so much," she said.

"That's why you need to remember, little one," the king replied. "You need to keep them alive in your thoughts and in your heart."

He pulled away from her, and she reluctantly let go. She was afraid to look at him because she felt ashamed of crying so much. But he put his hand on her chin and gently raised her head to look into his face. He was smiling, and the look he gave her made Annie know that it was okay for her to let him see her like this.

"Thank you for telling me your story, little hedgehog," he said.

Annie found herself almost laughing at his pet name for her. She really did feel like a little hedgehog sometimes, all rolled up with her spikes sticking out so that no one could really get too close. Her costume had been more appropriate than she'd realized when she'd made it. But the king had made her abandon that armor, and she felt a lot better for it.

"What you told me could not have been easy for you," said the Oak King.

"No," said Annie, "it wasn't easy." She didn't tell him that she'd never told anyone else that story. Even her aunt didn't know that she had been the one who had left the Christmas tree lights plugged in. Annie had never been able to tell her.

"I think, though, that you are too hard on yourself," the king continued. "Death, like everything else, is ultimately a part of life. Is that not what we learn from walking the path? Is that not what you learned tonight from my battle with my brother?"

Annie sniffled. It was true, death and life *were* all part of the cycle of things. Her involvement in Wicca had taught her that time and time again. Things changed—the seasons, the moon, the tides.

The wheel turned and turned again. That's what celebrating the sabbats was all about. And death was most definitely a big part of the cycle. But knowing that didn't make this particular part of her life any easier. Accepting life and death as a cycle was okay for dealing with things like animals' dying and gardens' decaying, but it didn't change the fact that her parents had died because of something she'd done. People were more important than animals and flowers. Their deaths meant more.

She thought about Elizabeth Sanger, the girl from school who had been killed two months before. Helping to find and catch her killer had made Annie feel better, but she didn't think it had made accepting the fact that Elizabeth had been murdered any easier to take, especially for the people who had loved her. Death just hurt. Accepting it turned the hurt into a different kind of pain, but it didn't make it go away.

Her parents' deaths were part of her life. She couldn't change that. But thinking of their deaths as part of some overall cosmic plan didn't heal the wound inside of her. That would always be there. If she understood the Oak King correctly, he was suggesting that she should somehow accept what happened to them as part of *her* path. Could she do that? She didn't know. It was a lot to ask.

But maybe I can, she thought as she looked from the Oak King to the Holly King. *Maybe that's my challenge*.

The Oak King stood up and stretched. "Now that I'm awake, I think it's time you joined the world again," he said to Annie. "There's a party waiting for you."

"I'm sorry I made such a fool of myself," Annie said to the two kings as they led her out of the room. "I know I must look like some kind of lunatic to you."

"Not at all," the Oak King said. "You look like one who has experienced the power of Midsummer. You don't have to tell *me* how strong that power can be."

He laughed then, and Annie found that it made her feel much better. It reminded her of living, and of good times, and she needed that right then. There had been a lot of death in the evening's activities. Now she thought she understood the purpose of it, but she needed to do something to take her mind away from it. She wanted to dance.

"I should find my friends and get ready for the midnight dance," she said. "Can you take me to them?"

"That we can," said the Holly King, opening the door of the little chamber and ushering her through.

She and the kings walked up the stone steps. When they reached the door at the top, the Holly King took the blindfold out once more and tied it around Annie's eyes. He took her hand and led her to the door. Again she heard a door opening, and then someone helped her through. Then it was a long walk in silence as they wound their way through the woods.

After a while the king took Annie's blindfold off. She looked around. Even in the dark she saw that she was somewhere sort of familiar. A path stretched out in front of them, and the king pointed down it.

"Down that way you will find the mortal world," the Oak King said, sounding very mysterious. "I believe you will find what you are looking for there. Go to them. But do not speak to anyone of what you have seen tonight. It was for your eyes alone."

Annie turned to the Holly King. "I'm sorry I was kind of a jerk earlier," she said. "I know this was all just part of the game."

"No offense was taken, little hedgehog," the Holly King said. "My brother was lucky to have you by his side. I should hope for such a fearless squire when my turn comes to die."

"Well, you never know," Annie said. "I might just come back and find you."

With that she turned and walked away, leaving the Holly King and the Oak King to return to the forest as she walked down the path to the Midsummer dance.

CHAPTER 17

"Come on. We're going to miss it if we don't hurry."

Kate sat up. Tyler was standing above her, pulling on her arm. What was going on? Where was she? She looked around and saw that she was still in the woods. Then she remembered—she'd been dancing. But where were they? Where was Maeve? She rubbed her eyes, trying to clear her head.

"Kate, come *on*," Tyler said. "What kind of faerie princess are you, falling asleep before the Midsummer dance?"

"But we *were* dancing," Kate said. "Don't you remember? I picked you. I picked you over the others."

"Well, you've been having a little nap since then," Tyler said teasingly. "I guess the dancing was a little too much excitement."

"I went looking for you," Kate explained. "You were dressed as a raven. Then I met Maeve and there was this faun and then—"

"I think you've been dreaming," Tyler said, laughing.

"But it happened!" she said. "I remember everything: the masks, and the dancing, and Scott."

"Scott?" Tyler said. "You dreamed about Scott?"

Kate looked at Tyler. Did he really not remember what had happened? Worse, had she dreamed it all somehow?

"But you were the one I picked," said Kate again, trying to get him to admit that it wasn't her imagination. "You're the one I love."

She stopped as soon as she said the words. Tyler was looking at her, a peculiar expression on his face. "What did you say?" he asked.

Kate couldn't take it back. She'd said what she'd been thinking of saying all night. And now that she'd actually done it, she knew that it was true. She really did love Tyler. She'd been afraid to admit that, but her experiences in the woods had made her see that it was how she really felt.

"I said I love you," she said again, standing up and facing Tyler.

"That's what I thought you said," Tyler replied. "I just wanted to make sure."

Kate felt her heart racing. She'd just told her boyfriend that she loved him. More than that, she'd said it and she'd *believed* it. It wasn't just something to say because she thought she had to. It was something she felt inside. But did Tyler feel it, too, or had she made a huge mistake? She looked at his face, waiting for a response.

Tyler took her in his arms and pulled her to

him. "I thought I'd be the first one to say that," he said. "In fact, I was looking for you so I could. But since you beat me to it, I'll have to settle for being a copycat. I love you, too, Kate."

He kissed her, his mouth closing over hers and his arms pulling her to him. As they stood there in each other's arms, Kate didn't care whether the events of the night had been a dream or not. It didn't matter. What mattered was that she and Tyler were in love. But where had Scott gone? Maybe he was out there somewhere, camping with his friends. She didn't care. What had happened with Scott on the beach wasn't important now. She had told Tyler that she loved him—and he had said it back.

"They're starting the dance," Tyler said as they let one another go. "Let's go."

He took Kate's hand and pulled her down the path toward the music. She hurried along, eager to join the fun and anxious to see her friends so she could tell them what had happened.

Cooper stormed through the woods. She couldn't believe the night she'd had. This was one Midsummer she wanted to forget, and soon. She'd been dragged through the woods, put through a weird ritual, and then abandoned by the people who had staged the whole thing. What was wrong with these guys? This wasn't how Wicca was supposed to work. She wanted to find Archer and

Sophia and give them a piece of her mind. It was one thing to throw some surprises their way, but it was another to chase them through the woods. She didn't want any part of it. She didn't like being thrown into situations beyond her control.

Now all she wanted to do was get out of the woods, find her friends, and be done with it. She'd had enough of faeries and Midsummer and, frankly, magic to last her about a hundred years. If she never heard another "blessed be" or "merry meet" it would be fine with her. She didn't want to dance. She didn't want to play dress-up. She just wanted to be left alone.

She wasn't sure where she was going. She'd run out of the cave and into the woods without really thinking about it. But now she heard music. It wasn't the same kind of music that Bird, Spider, and the others had been playing. It was ordinary music—good but nothing special. That was one thing she had to admit about what had happened, the music had been fantastic. She didn't know where those kids had learned to play like that, but they were amazing. If only they hadn't been so weird, and if only she didn't feel so angry, she might actually try to find them and play with them. But she *was* angry, and she wasn't going to calm down any time soon.

She walked in the direction of the music. Although she didn't have any interest now in joining the remaining festivities, she knew that Annie and

Kate would be at the dance. She wanted to find them so she could tell them what had happened to her. There was something else she wanted to tell them, but they weren't going to like that part very much.

Annie couldn't wait to find Cooper and Kate and tell them all about her night. Everything had been so real, so vivid. She'd experienced things that she would never forget. Best of all, she had begun to accept some things about herself, and about her parents, that she'd been keeping hidden for far too long. Her time with the Oak King and the Holly King had showed her that she needed to remember. She needed to remember her mother and her father, and she had to remember how much they had loved her and how much she had loved them. She had to stop hiding from the past and learn to accept it, as difficult as that was to do.

Her mind was almost bursting with new thoughts and new feelings. She couldn't believe how perfect the ritual had been. It was as if it had been created especially for her. How had they known what she needed? How had they staged everything so carefully, so beautifully? Everything had been just right, from the costumes to the performances by the various actors. She didn't even like to think of them as actors. They'd seemed so real to her, so alive. She wanted to remember them as the characters they had played, as the Oak King and the Holly King. She couldn't think of them as just ordinary men in costumes. They meant more to her than that.

She thought of all the things she wanted to do when she got home. She wanted to ask her aunt about her father and mother. She wanted to talk about them and about their lives. She wanted to find out more about her mother's artwork. There were so many things she didn't know because she'd been afraid to ask, afraid that talking about them would mean telling someone that she felt responsible for her parents' deaths. But now that she had told someone she knew that she could do it again.

She would start by telling Kate and Cooper, though. They were her best friends. They were like sisters. Even more important, they were a circle. Magic tied them together. It was something they shared, and it was something that was as important to her as blood. As she neared the clearing where the dance was, she knew that more than anything she wanted to see them and tell them everything.

Kate, Cooper, and Annie entered the ritual area at the same time, but from different parts of the woods. It took them a minute to find one another in the crowd of people who filled the clearing. The bustle of the bodies made it hard to move, but each made her way to the same place to one side of the festivities.

"You won't believe what I've been doing," Annie said happily.

"No, you won't believe what *I've* been doing," Cooper said gruffly.

"Well, neither of you will believe what I said to Tyler," said Kate dreamily.

For a moment they all spoke at the same time, tripping over one another's words until Cooper held up her hands. "One at a time," she said. "Annie, you first."

"I was part of this really cool play sort of thing," she said. "Some of it was really sad and really hard, but mostly it was fantastic. I don't know how they did it. Where were you guys?"

"I was in the woods chasing Tyler around," Kate said sheepishly. "It's hard to explain. But I met the Faerie Queen and ran into Scott and this guy dressed like a faun. Then I had to pick one of them to be my true love. It's all kind of weird. The important thing is that I told Tyler I love him."

"You did not," Cooper said, momentarily forgetting her own story.

Kate nodded. "I did," she said. "And he said it back. This has been the *best* Midsummer night ever."

Hearing her friends' excitement, Cooper wasn't sure she wanted to tell them about her experience. They both seemed to have had great times. Had the ritual she'd become part of simply gone wrong? She couldn't tell. But either way, she had made a decision.

"Um, I have to tell you guys something," she said.

Kate and Annie looked at her expectantly. She knew they were waiting for her to share some great story about her evening.

"It's not quite as great as what you guys said," Cooper told them.

Behind them, the music was growing louder. People were forming a circle, and Tyler was calling for Kate.

"Come on, Cooper. The dance is about to start," Kate said. "What did you want to tell us?"

Cooper sighed. "I don't think I want to be in the group anymore," she said.

follow the
circle ᗝf three

with book 6:
Ring of Light

"Come on," Kate said, grabbing Tyler's hand and pulling him up the front walk to her house. "It's not going to be that bad."

"Easy for you to say," Tyler joked as he followed along behind her. "You're not the one spending the day with your girlfriend's parents for the first time."

Kate stopped at the door and turned to look at her boyfriend. His black hair was, as usual, tousled but adorable, and his eyes, a peculiar deep gold color, sparkled in the July sun. Her parents had met Tyler a few times and seemed to like him, but she was still a little nervous. This was the first time they'd all be together for more than half an hour. Tyler was the first guy she'd brought home since Scott, and they'd thought that Scott was the perfect boyfriend for her. They hadn't understood when she broke things off with him, and she knew that might make them particularly critical of Tyler, who

213

had replaced Scott as the guy in her life.

"Don't worry," she said, reassuring herself as much as she was reassuring Tyler. "They're going to *love* you."

Tyler grinned. "That would be nice," he said, "but the only one I need to love me is you."

Kate rolled her eyes, but inside she was thrilled to hear Tyler say that. Only recently had either of them said the L-word, and it was still new to her. Every time Tyler said it, she felt like she was the most important person in the world.

"I do love you," she said, leaning up and kissing him.

Just as their lips met, the front door opened and her father's face appeared.

"Am I interrupting something?" he said gruffly.

Startled, Kate pulled away from her boyfriend and instinctively wiped her hand across her mouth in embarrassment.

"Hi, Daddy," she said, trying to keep her composure.

"Hello, Mr. Morgan," Tyler said, doing a much better job than Kate was of pretending that they hadn't just been caught making out. "It's nice to see you again."

Mr. Morgan reached out and took Tyler's offered hand, shaking it firmly while looking his daughter's boyfriend up and down carefully. "Nice to see you again, too," he said evenly.

Avoiding her father's gaze, Kate slipped past

him and into the house, drawing Tyler after her. She hustled him through the living room and into the kitchen, where her mother was rushing around doing ten different things at once as she prepared the food for the cookout they were having.

"Hi, honey," Mrs. Morgan said as she turned from checking something in the oven and went back to chopping celery at the counter.

When she saw Tyler standing behind her daughter she stopped what she was doing and smiled at him. "Hi, Tyler," she said. "I'd shake hands but I'm afraid they're covered in barbeque sauce, flour, and who knows what else."

"That's okay," Tyler said. "I get the idea, and whatever it is you're cooking, it smells amazing, so the trade-off is more than worth it."

Mrs. Morgan looked at Kate. "This one's a flatterer," she said. "Watch out for those. They'll get you every time. I should know—it's how your father got me."

Kate blushed. "Well, everything does smell great," she said, trying to change the subject. "What's on the menu?"

"The usual Fourth of July picnic spread," her mother replied. "Hot dogs, fried chicken, corn on the cob, potato salad, baked beans, and chocolate cake."

"I smell something else," Kate said, sniffing the air around the oven. She opened the door and peeked inside, where she saw a pan of lasagna sitting on one of the racks.

"Lasagna?" she said suspiciously. "You only make lasagna when—"

"When Kyle's home?" a voice behind her finished.

Kate wheeled around, letting out a squeal of surprise when she saw her older brother standing there, a huge grin on his face and his arms held open. She ran to him and wrapped her arms around him as he picked her up and swung her around.

"What are you doing here?" she asked when he finally put her down. "I thought you were staying at the university this summer to work."

"I am," Kyle said. "But I have a little time off. Besides, I had to bring you something."

"Bring me something?" Kate said. "What do you mean?"

"Oh, it's just a little present I picked up on the way here," Kyle answered mysteriously. "Want to see it? It's out back."

Kate looked at her mother, who was also now grinning wickedly.

"Do you know about this?" Kate asked her.

"You'll just have to go and see for yourself," her mother said, pretending to be busy ripping up lettuce for a salad.

Kate headed for the back door with everyone following behind her. She had no idea what Kyle could be talking about. It wasn't her birthday or anything, and she was surprised enough to see him home for the Fourth. What else could he have brought with him?

She burst through the screen door and stepped into the backyard, looking around for her big surprise. What she saw was the barbeque, the coals already glowing, and a picnic table piled with paper plates and plastic utensils. Then she noticed that someone was sitting in one of the lawn chairs that had been set out. When she realized who it was, she gasped.

"Aunt Netty?" she said, not believing her eyes.

"The one and only," said the woman in the chair as she stood up. "Surprised?"

Kate darted forward and hugged her aunt tightly, all the while laughing with delight. She couldn't believe it—her favorite aunt was standing in her backyard.

"I told you I picked up something you would like," Kyle said teasingly.

Kate turned to Tyler, who was standing in the doorway silently watching the goings-on. "This is my Aunt Netty," she said happily.

"I got that part," Tyler quipped. He stepped forward and shook the woman's hand. "I'm Tyler," he told her.

Aunt Netty raised an eyebrow and turned to her niece. "Not bad at all," she said. "I see you inherited the Rampling women's good taste in men."

She turned back to Tyler and smiled. "Don't take me too seriously," she said. "I'm just teasing."

"No problem," Tyler responded. "I happen to think Kate has pretty good taste in men myself."

Everyone laughed at his joke. Kate, who still hadn't let go of her aunt's hand, was looking at her closely. "You cut your hair," she said. "It used to hang down past your shoulders."

Aunt Netty shook her head. She was wearing a straw hat, and her hair barely touched her shoulders. "I didn't like all of that hair hanging in my face," she said. "Do you like the new look? I think it's kind of Audrey Hepburn in *Breakfast at Tiffany's*."

"Sure," Kate answered. "Now, tell me how long you're here for. I suppose it's just for the weekend, right?"

"That's the best part of the surprise," her aunt said. "I'm here for a longer visit this time."

Kate couldn't believe her good luck. Not only was her favorite aunt there, she was going to stay for a while. "A week?" she asked hopefully.

"At least," said her aunt. "It depends on how things go with the project I'm working on."

"This is so great," Kate exclaimed. "What better way to spend the Fourth of July than with my favorite people?"

"How about *eating* with your favorite people?" her father suggested as he came out with a platter piled high with hot dogs and headed for the grill. "I think your mother could use a hand bringing the rest of that food out here."

"Let's go make ourselves useful," Aunt Netty suggested to Kate.

"You just sit down, Netty," Mr. Morgan said. "The kids can help Teresa."

Aunt Netty groaned and made a face at Kate's father. "Whatever you say, Joe," she said, and sank back into the lawn chair.

Kate went back into the kitchen, taking Tyler with her. Inside, she loaded him up with things to carry, all the while talking about her aunt.

"She's my mom's little sister," she informed him as she handed him a big bowl of chips. "She's really funny, and she's a photographer. She's always going somewhere different to shoot for magazines. Wait until you see her stuff. She must be here on some kind of assignment."

"She seems really nice," Tyler said, trying to juggle all the things Kate was handing him.

"You can make more than one trip, you know," her mother said.

"Sorry," said Kate, realizing that she'd overloaded her boyfriend and taking back the napkins she'd tried to squeeze under his arm. "I'm just so excited about Aunt Netty being here."

They went back outside, where Tyler helped Kate arrange things on the picnic table. When everything was ready, the whole family gathered around and began loading up their plates. Mr. Morgan stood by the grill, turning hot dogs and handing them out when they were done. Before long everyone was sitting in lawn chairs, happily eating and enjoying the beautiful sunny afternoon.

"This sure beats cafeteria food," Kyle said as he dug into his second piece of lasagna. "I think the university should hire you to cater for us, Mom."

"Your mother has enough business here to keep her working overtime," Mr. Morgan commented. "Don't give her any ideas. We hardly see her as it is."

"This really is amazing, Mrs. Morgan," Tyler said as he nibbled on an ear of corn. "I can't wait to try some of that cake."

"Do you want some potato salad, Aunt Netty?" Kate asked, glancing at her aunt's plate. "You haven't eaten very much."

"Thanks, sweetie," Aunt Netty replied. "I'm all set. It's all delicious, but like Tyler I'm trying to save room for that cake."

"That just means there's more for me," Kate said, getting up to refill her plate.

"So, Tyler, tell me about yourself," said Kate's aunt when Kate returned and settled back into her seat beside her boyfriend. "Where did you and Kate meet?"